Something Just Like This

Also From Jennifer Probst

The Stay Series
The Start of Something Good
A Brand New Ending
All Roads Lead to You

The Billionaire Builders
Everywhere and Every Way
Any Time, Any Place
All Or Nothing At All
Somehow, Some Way

Searching for Series:
Searching for Someday
Searching for Perfect
Searching for Beautiful
Searching for Always
Searching for You
Searching For Mine

The Marriage to a Billionaire series
The Marriage Bargain
The Marriage Trap
The Marriage Mistake
The Marriage Merger
The Marriage Arrangement
The Books of Spells

Executive Seduction

All the Way

The Sex on the Beach Series
Beyond Me
Chasing Me

The Hot in the Hamptons Series
Summer Sins

The Steele Brother Series
Catch Me
Play Me
Dare Me
Beg Me
Reveal Me

Dante's Fire
The Grinch of Starlight Bend

Something Just Like This

A Stay Novella

By Jennifer Probst

1001 Dark Nights

EVIL EYE
CONCEPTS

Something Just Like This
A Stay Novella
By Jennifer Probst

1001 Dark Nights

Copyright 2019 Triple J Publishing Inc
ISBN: 978-1-970077-20-9

Foreword: Copyright 2014 M. J. Rose

Published by Evil Eye Concepts, Incorporated

Acknowledgments from the Author

Thank you to Liz Berry, M.J. Rose, and Jillian Stein for allowing me to be part of this special 1001 Dark Nights family. I treasure every book.

Sign up for the 1001 Dark Nights Newsletter
and be entered to win a Tiffany Key necklace.

There's a contest every month!

Go to www.1001DarkNights.com to subscribe.

**As a bonus, all subscribers can download
FIVE FREE exclusive books!**

One Thousand and One Dark Nights

Once upon a time, in the future…

*I was a student fascinated with stories and learning.
I studied philosophy, poetry, history, the occult, and
the art and science of love and magic. I had a vast
library at my father's home and collected thousands
of volumes of fantastic tales.*

*I learned all about ancient races and bygone
times. About myths and legends and dreams of all
people through the millennium. And the more I read
the stronger my imagination grew until I discovered
that I was able to travel into the stories... to actually
become part of them.*

*I wish I could say that I listened to my teacher
and respected my gift, as I ought to have. If I had, I
would not be telling you this tale now.
But I was foolhardy and confused, showing off
with bravery.*

*One afternoon, curious about the myth of the
Arabian Nights, I traveled back to ancient Persia to
see for myself if it was true that every day Shahryar
(Persian: : شهريار, "king") married a new virgin, and then
sent yesterday's wife to be beheaded. It was written
and I had read, that by the time he met Scheherazade,
the vizier's daughter, he'd killed one thousand
women.*

Something went wrong with my efforts. I arrived in the midst of the story and somehow exchanged places with Scheherazade — a phenomena that had never occurred before and that still to this day, I cannot explain.

Now I am trapped in that ancient past. I have taken on Scheherazade's life and the only way I can protect myself and stay alive is to do what she did to protect herself and stay alive.

Every night the King calls for me and listens as I spin tales. And when the evening ends and dawn breaks, I stop at a point that leaves him breathless and yearning for more. And so the King spares my life for one more day, so that he might hear the rest of my dark tale.

As soon as I finish a story... I begin a new one... like the one that you, dear reader, have before you now.

Chapter One

"I want you to run for governor."

Jonathan Lake stared down at his clasped hands as the fateful words echoed in his head. Less than an hour ago, he'd had a closed-door meeting with the current governor, who informed him he was not seeking re-election. It'd be a shock to the party, but they'd already focused in on the candidate they believed had a solid shot at winning.

Him.

Oh, the shit was about to hit the proverbial fan. Once the story got out, it'd be a shark-feeding frenzy with him smack in the middle of the red waters. Did he really want this? He'd only been mayor for one term and was just beginning to settle into the job. New York City was a dirty bastard, but he loved every grimy, fierce, beautiful inch of it, from the concrete to the skyscrapers. Was he even ready to move on and take on the entire state?

His late wife's voice whispered in his ear, even after all these years.

This is what you were meant for.

Pushing his fingers through his hair, he got up from his chair and began to pace his office. Thoughts whirled in his head, making him feel as if he'd overindulged in martinis at lunch. So much to think about. He'd call his daughter Chloe and get her feedback. And, of course, Mia, who handled his PR. He'd tell Bob, his campaign manager, in the morning. The former marine would be working his ass off nonstop for the next year—might as well give him one last evening free. But there was one woman on his mind. One who not only ran his schedule but also his entire life. The woman he trusted as fiercely as he did Chloe and Mia.

He strode over to the desk and hit the button. "Can you come in here, please?"

The clipped, cool voice echoed in the air. "Of course."

He counted down the eight seconds it always took her to move from her desk to his office, and the door opened on cue. She entered with the smooth, assured stride he'd memorized and slid into her chair opposite his desk, her tablet held between tapered fingers with short, naked nails. She wore her usual black pantsuit and low-heeled black pumps. Once he'd joked if she had seven identical pantsuits in her closet for each day of the week.

She'd said they were all black, but not identical because they were different designers and fabric, and she kept an eighth outfit available for emergencies. She didn't understand jokes very well. Her sense of humor was Spock-like, and it had taken him a while to get used to it.

He stared at the nape of her neck, exposed from the ruthless topknot she kept her ash-blond hair tied in, her gaze trained on the screen in front of her. He knew the gaze well. Big, brown eyes hidden behind smart, tortoiseshell-framed glasses. Razor-focused. Ruthlessly composed. Sharply intelligent. A bit distant.

And endlessly fascinating.

"No notes," he clipped out, resuming his pacing. "I need to discuss something with you."

"He wants you to run for governor."

He jerked, then wondered why he was surprised. Her IQ wasn't just off the charts on paper, but she could also read people. The combination made her the best damn right-hand person he'd ever employed in his life. It also made her completely irreplaceable—and she knew it.

"Yes. He's decided not to run for re-election and thinks I can win."

She never tried to turn her head to gaze at him, allowing him to pace his office like the cage it sometimes was. Her aura seeped a calmness that already soothed the wild chatter in his mind. She was almost witchlike in her ability to give him whatever he needed. Maybe that was why he'd begun thinking of her as much more than his assistant and advisor.

Or maybe he was finally starting to break under his long-imposed years of celibacy.

"You can win," she said. "Statistically, you're the best choice. Your approval ratings are top-rated. You're coming off a victory of reducing the amount of homelessness in the city, and your political views are balanced so the liberals and conservatives will both be satisfied. You're a dream candidate, Mr. Mayor, and our governor has never been stupid. He endorses you, steps out of the spotlight, and gives you a clear path to victory."

"Stop calling me that," he barked, irritation prickling his skin. "We're alone. I told you this before."

She inclined her head with grace. "Sorry, Jonathan."

His name on her tongue calmed the beast. He dropped into his leather chair and drummed his fingers on the table, staring at her. She stared back, unblinking, waiting patiently for whatever he wanted to throw at her.

Damnit. He'd hired her because she knew her shit, came highly recommended, and they'd never want to sleep with each other. His last hire had been a mistake, one who ended up crushing on him and failing at her job. His long-term assistant had finally succumbed to retirement, and he'd been floundering at the loss. The moment Alyssa Block had walked into his office with her cool eyes and clipped speech, he'd known they weren't each other's types. He preferred fiery, opinionated, passionate women like his beloved late wife. A partner who challenged him mentally and physically. It was also obvious that Alyssa didn't give a crap about flirting with him or being physical—she just wanted to do her job the best she could.

That had been over two years ago, and they'd been inseparable ever since. In a good way.

He'd learned early on that mixing business with personal relationships meant disaster—any politician who wanted a career knew the rules to follow. History proved itself over and over. Men who couldn't keep their pants zipped made for crappy leaders. He didn't get involved in opinions, whether it was right or wrong for his personal life to be scrutinized and judged. Jonathan only dealt with the facts, and if he couldn't change them or tweak them, acceptance was the best route.

He never thought it'd be a problem. Until lately.

Because, lately, he'd been thinking about Alyssa in many more ways than as his assistant. And it was wrecking the entire orderly world that she so competently managed for him.

"I planned to run for another term. There's still so much more to do."

"This is an opportunity you may not get again. You can do more as governor."

He drummed faster. She gave a tiny sigh, then pushed the red stress ball over the polished mahogany. It had been a Christmas present from his daughter—embedded with the term Mayoral Tension Reliever—and he'd been crushing it ever since, like a dog gnawing on a favorite bone. He began squeezing, and the give under his fingers took him down a notch. "Or I may get less done. You know the higher up the ladder, the less you make a difference."

"If that's what you believe. Staying mayor will be an easier route."

He snorted, cutting her a glance. "Trying to challenge my ego to get me to run?"

"We need less ego in politics, Jonathan. Not more."

He raised a brow. "Well said."

"You were the one who said it."

"Damn, I'm good."

The slight tug at her bottom lip made him feel as if he'd won *American Ninja Warrior*. The woman didn't smile often, but when she did, it was like a gift. And why the hell was he concentrating on that ridiculous thought?

"It'll be hell on Earth once we make the announcement. I almost lost my daughter over the mayoral election. I can't lose myself like that again."

Ah, he had regrets. He'd been so focused on being mayor after moving on from his position as district attorney that he'd ignored her needs, chalking it up to teen angst. Instead, she'd been crying for his attention, the loss of her mother still tearing her apart. Jonathan had been able to bury the grief deep enough and soothe it with work. But Chloe had needed to talk, and feel, and do all that *girl* stuff that was important but that he mostly sucked at. Looking back, he realized what an ass he'd been, and he'd sworn to always put her first from now on.

He waited for sympathy but, of course, Alyssa only shrugged. "That was then. This is now. Mia's a crackerjack and will get you through. Bob's a pro and got you here. Chloe's in a solid place with her career and no longer as raw. You've both grown." She narrowed her gaze. "Do you want it? Aside from the rush of power being governor will bring? Because, if you don't, that's where it will all go wrong."

She was right. It was hard chipping past the amazing adrenaline blast of imagining himself as governor of New York State. He squeezed the ball and really looked inward and swore not to flinch. He liked being respected. Loved having big-time contacts and the ability to change things. But did he want this for himself and his career, or did he believe this new course could make the state a better place?

He thought of Chloe, and his late wife, Catherine, and the people he fought for daily knowing he'd only succeed in a fraction of what he wanted to accomplish. It was a path of bitter disappointment and heartbreaking cynicism. But, God, he wanted a chance to try. To be a better man. To push himself to think of the people's needs instead of his ability to get a reservation at the hottest restaurants and schmooze with DC royalty.

No. He wanted more for everyone. And he'd regret it if he didn't try.

He opened his mouth to tell her his decision.

"Good choice," she said, her fingers tapping on the tablet screen. "I'll schedule a meeting with Mia and Bob. Chloe said she'd be back in her office at two p.m., so I'll text her you'll be calling then. I'll make a list of contacts you need to reach out to immediately—I assume you're canceling dinner with Jack at Carmine's tonight?"

He winced. "Ah, hell, I forgot. He's the most boring man I've ever met. It's like a disease."

"Cherophobia," she stated.

He tilted his head. "What?"

"The fear of fun. That's what Jack probably has."

He laughed. She was always spouting off strange and interesting facts, her brain an amazing apparatus that fascinated him. Too many women bored him after one dinner conversation. Alyssa had been challenging him regularly, so in a way, he'd been spoiled. "Finally, a true diagnosis I can understand."

"I'll cite a work emergency and order dinner in with the team." She continued her endless checklist, making notes, shifting events, and taking care of what he needed before he knew he needed it. By the time she rose from the chair, the stress ball was resting still on the desk, and his mind was once again lasered in and settled. He caught a gentle whiff of her perfume—some clean, fresh-cotton scent. Or linen? In the beginning, it had struck him as no-nonsense, barely able to be called a cologne. Now, he took a deep breath and savored the smell. It reminded him of cool, soft sheets on naked skin. Non-flashy but memorable. They spent endless hours together, yet he still hadn't cracked the essence of her—the core hidden behind the unbreakable shell.

For a long time, he hadn't cared. It hadn't mattered because they were good together. A perfect team who worked like a well-oiled machine.

Now, he craved more. To know the woman she was when she left the office. Who she loved and trusted. What she really wanted.

She paused as if sensing his sudden unease from his intimate thoughts. "Are you okay, Mr. Mayor?"

She wasn't the type for red lipstick and preferred a rose gloss that gave just a hint of color and sheen. Sweat broke out on his skin as he suddenly imagined his mouth on hers, the gasp he'd swallow as his tongue dove deep, the bite of her nails in his shoulders, the feel of her tight body pressed against his.

He tore his gaze away and quickly swiveled his chair around, desperate to hide his sudden, alarming interest in his assistant. He needed to get his shit together. The campaign for governor was going to be long and hard, with cramped quarters and countless hours spent together. This was not the time to fall apart over a woman he'd known for two years, and who would quit and run screaming out of his life if she knew he was suddenly imagining her naked.

He'd fix it. Control it. Rationalize it away. Whatever he needed to do because now he had one goal.

Win.

Chapter Two

Things were getting worse.

Alyssa poured the wine to well over her usual quarter-glass and curled up on the comfy white lounge chair. She ignored the remote and switched her cell to silent. Even the fresh stack of books beside her, spines ramrod straight, pages crisp and untouched, couldn't tempt her. Right now, she just wanted to rest in the quiet of her apartment and go over the day's shocking events.

He was going to be governor.

Pride rippled through her, along with a longing that was beginning to peek through her solidly built walls. She had no doubt he'd win. Jonathan Lake was the perfect trifecta in the voting world—looks, charisma, and heart. She didn't respect many politicians and rarely offered her skillset to anyone she didn't admire. With her ruthless organization skills and the need to remain hidden from the spotlight, she'd worked with high-profile lawyers, government officials, and television producers. But when she'd heard that Lake was desperate for a trained assistant, she'd taken the leap for an interview.

Alyssa shivered and took a bigger gulp of wine. God, the man was all sexiness and heat—from his smooth, velvety voice to his lean, pantherlike body clothed in power suits. The thick, coal-black hair, chiseled jaw, and piercing blue eyes could hold the attention of any person, whether man or woman. His energy sizzled and practically lit up the room with intensity. But Alyssa had been prepared. She was used to charm and good looks.

She'd grown up in the performance world, where egos and physical attributes usually outweighed kindness and the actual desire to help others. She'd never expected to like Jonathan or take the job.

Wrong on both counts.

He'd interviewed her with a cool ruthlessness she admired, trying to unearth every foible and weakness to carefully judge if she was good enough to work for him. She'd expected a touch of chauvinism and the easy, flirty manner of most attractive men in power.

Not him. It was obvious that the man wanted nothing to do with her on that level, and even if he did, she doubted he had the time. He'd offered her the job on the spot, and she'd taken it, sensing it was the right move for both of them.

That had been just over two years ago. How had she gotten into this mess? When had she begun to fall for the mayor of New York City—her boss?

A groan escaped her lips. If only she were able to pinpoint when mutual respect had turned. When she suddenly looked at him, exhausted from twelve-hour days, and saw a man she wanted to touch rather than the mayor she wanted to help. She was stringent about keeping her bodily reactions in check, and an expert at masking any type of emotion so he'd never know.

But she did, and it was humiliating. She was hot for him. Dreamt a million fantasies of office sex on his desk, even the clichéd ones where he pushed everything to the floor and ravaged her right there on the hard, unyielding wood. Why did she have to be so damn unoriginal?

On cue, her phone vibrated. Of course, it was probably him. He always texted when she was vulnerable. Alone in her big, empty apartment, thinking of him naked.

She steeled herself and grabbed her cell, then found it was much worse. The man had not only mesmerized her when she'd believed herself invincible to his charm, but he'd also managed to up the stakes.

He'd gotten her to fall in love with his daughter.

Alyssa tapped the button. "Hi, Chloe. How are you?"

"Oh, my God, I heard the news. I cannot believe he's running for governor. Alyssa, do you think it's too soon? He said he always wanted at least two terms as mayor, and now he'll be thrown into another election. I'm worried."

"Well, I assume you talked about the options at length with him, but I believe it's an opportunity he can't pass up."

A sigh came over the phone. "I know. It's just a lot more pressure and longer hours."

Alyssa heard the hesitation in Chloe's voice. "Are you worried about what happened before?" she asked gently.

"A little. I mean, I know we're better now. I'm no longer a college student, pissed off and vandalizing cars for attention," she joked. "But what if he gets too wrapped up in the voting results again? He was stressed and unhappy, Alyssa. And since my mom, he hasn't focused on anything but his career. It's not good for him."

Alyssa's heart squeezed. The past two years, she'd gotten to know Chloe, both from her father's stories and her own personal experience with the girl. She was a younger, female version of Jonathan with gorgeous black hair, beautiful blue eyes, and an enthusiastic personality and energy that swept through the room like a tidal wave. She'd graduated from SUNY New Paltz with a business degree, then began working with a local organization to advocate for stronger anti-cruelty laws for animals. Her passion for public service was evident in her job and her volunteer work with animal rescue farms in the county. The two of them were like a dynamic duo, ready to rule the world. But with that commitment for change came the tendency to get so wrapped up in the mechanics one lost sight of the true goal.

Still, she believed what she'd told Jonathan. They were both older and stronger now, and Alyssa knew he'd handle things better this time around. "If your father goes off course, you'll set him straight. He can't push you around like before. I won't let him."

Chloe laughed. "If anyone can handle Dad, it's you. Just make sure you let me know if he needs an intervention. When does the announcement go live?"

"Next week. If we do a press conference on Tuesday, can you attend? He'd love to have you by his side."

"I'll make it work."

"Great, he'll be happy." They chatted a bit more about casual topics, then said goodbye. Alyssa finished her wine, savoring the silence, and wondered if she should get a cat. Maybe another presence in her life other than Jonathan and his daughter would help. Cats were independent, right? With her crazy work schedule, she'd never believed it was fair to bring an animal here. But a distraction might be needed, along with an excuse to retreat during those late-night war sessions he planned too much. She was always vulnerable then. Watching him plow his fingers through his mussed hair, his tie and jacket shed, his eyes crinkling with weariness in his need to save the city. How many times had she fought the urge to cross the room and cradle him in her arms? To soothe and comfort and be close?

It was dangerous for both of them. She had to get herself under control, or she'd be forced to make a heartbreaking decision.

She'd have to quit and leave forever.

Alyssa dragged in a breath and placed her lone glass in the sink. The only sound was the hum of the air conditioner. She padded on bare feet toward her bedroom, wondering when the silence had changed from comforting to lonely.

Definitely dangerous.

She'd get a cat this week.

Chapter Three

City Hall was a massive brick building that was the oldest in the United States, and one of the largest government structures in the world. Besides the mayoral office, it housed the New York Council and thirteen municipal agencies under Jonathan's direction. The historical significance struck him hard every time he went to work, reminding him of his responsibilities to the people, and the humbling achievement of a dream he'd set long ago with his wife by his side.

Of course, he'd never imagined he'd be alone once he arrived at City Hall.

He'd also never envisioned the isolation and loneliness he'd feel amidst the masses of people who consistently surrounded him. From reporters, drivers, bodyguards, and endless staff, there was no such thing as privacy or alone time. When he was working toward becoming mayor, he'd buried his grief in the drive to win and nearly lost the man he'd once been with his wife and daughter. Now he'd learned to become more human, but with that came a touch of vulnerability and a slight resentment of the constant pressure and fishbowl lifestyle he'd once been thrilled to take on.

Crap, he was getting old.

He smothered an indulgent sigh as the car pulled up to the curb. It'd been a few weeks since he'd made the announcement, and he'd been running nonstop on the hamster wheel ever since. He gazed out the tinted windows at the rain-slicked pavement. Late fall in the city was a tricky thing. It was different from the beauty of the Hudson Valley a scant two hours away. New Yorkers faced seasonal changes like stoic soldiers going into battle—flicking up the collars on their fashionable coats to brave the wind, and donning designer boots to stomp through puddles with sheer determination, refusing to be late to the next event on their schedule. Between the temperamental weather, endless leaves blocking up the sewers, and the scurry to build up enough supplies to protect the roads during the long winter, Jonathan had always preferred the silent, sticky summers instead. Still, a long walk in Central Park reminded him that crisp air, burnt-orange stately trees, and the golden light that poured from the sky needed to be appreciated before the craze of the holiday season descended. "Thanks, Tim. I heard it was your anniversary. How many years?"

The older man lit up. "I can't believe you remembered, sir. Thirty-five, and feels like just yesterday. She wants to renew our vows in Vegas with Elvis at our side."

He laughed. "Do it. Nothing like the King for pure romance superpower." He pressed a card into the man's hand. "Here's something for both of you. Go out to a nice dinner."

His long-term driver jerked back. "Sir, you didn't have to. Thank you."

"Welcome. See you in a few."

He nodded and hurried into the building, ducking his head against the wind. He'd have to double-check on the weather report. Hurricane season still threatened, and he had to be careful about any impending trouble. God knew the state was still in disarray from Sandy, and that had been years ago.

"Mr. Mayor? May I have a word?"

He glanced over but didn't stop walking—every second was accounted for. "Ms. Delaney, to what do I owe the pleasure? Surely you don't need another colorful quote regarding my stance on school vaccinations or free lunches? I've been quite clear."

She fell in step beside him. "Crystal, Mr. Mayor. I'm more curious about your new beef with the police commissioner. Sources tell me you're at odds with his decision to protect a few good cops nearing retirement for some menial sins. Is everyone's pension at risk, or just Andrew Billings'?"

Ah, fuck. Diana Delaney was a reporter he'd initially despised, then resented, and, most recently, reluctantly admired. He hated the rag she worked for, but she'd proven to be endlessly stubborn in securing a comment and getting it right. He knew she was in the trenches and fiercely ambitious, so the respect came after she'd proven that she was above lying or tweaking the truth for good copy. He might not agree with her spins, but he believed in freedom of the press and all that came with it. The real problem was her damn sources and how they leaked gossip he wanted to keep a lid on.

He gave an easy laugh, though he knew she wouldn't be fooled. "The commissioner and I do not have a beef, we were merely behind locked doors for a discussion. I agree and support him wholeheartedly on his decision to do a thorough investigation but keep Mr. Billings active."

"Even though you vowed to get the dirty cops off the street?" she asked shrewdly. She was petite but packed a punch with her wildly curly hair, trim figure, and dark eyes that always held a shark-like intensity.

He treated her to a full glance, his gloved hand gripping the door handle. "Internal affairs will do their job, and if Billings is deemed culpable, the commissioner and I will handle it together."

"By pressing charges?"

His smile faded. His previous job as the district attorney was a slippery slope. He'd been able to view things blacker and whiter in that position. But mayor? Yeah, he'd learned early on there were many shades of gray, and it had nothing to do with a good romance novel.

"Yes, if necessary, we will most definitely prosecute. Now, if you'll excuse me."

He shut the door as politely as possible and hurried to his corner of the world, greeting people as he walked, his mind furiously going over the implications of his push/pull with the head of police and the million other problems buzzing around in his head like angry bees.

He got stopped a few more times before he finally made it to his inner sanctum. Alyssa followed him in as he threw his briefcase on the littered table. "You have thirty minutes before your next meeting," she said crisply, opening his closet and displaying a few freshly pressed white shirts and jackets she always kept on hand. "I have the new agenda for the town hall meeting ready for approval. Here are your messages."

He already knew they were ranked by most shit-worthy, and she took care of everything else. He quickly sifted through them, re-arranging meetings and addressing hot buttons of concern as he tore off his damp, wrinkled jacket before deciding that his shirt should go, too. Alyssa kept battering commands and questions at him, her back politely turned as usual.

"Thanks for the head's up on Tim's anniversary," he managed to interrupt. "How do you know all this stuff?"

"It's my job. Keeping a schedule is simple. Most people enjoy sharing dates of joy." As usual, she brushed off any type of compliment he tried to give her. He'd learned early on that her sense of accomplishment came from her own high standards and not anyone else's. She rattled on. "Mia said the Billings story has the potential to blow. I scheduled a call for her to go over the details so she can direct the social media campaign in the right direction."

"Yeah, well, Delaney torpedoed me on my way in. Seems she knows I had words with the commissioner about this. I don't know why he wants to protect Billings so hard. There's been soft proof floating around a while, and it's time I nail the guy and make him an example. For God's sake, there's enough dirt and drugs in my city without my police force contributing." The NYPD was stellar, and he was damn proud of their amazing accomplishments. He supported them, cheered them, and tried to protect most of them from the crap people who wanted to use or exploit them for political agendas. But Billings was just bad news—the exception rather than the rule. He needed to take care of it.

Her gaze swung around, almond eyes wide behind her glasses. "How'd Diana find out? She got a mole on the inside finally?"

He couldn't help the half-grin that lifted his lips. "Probably. Or she went to Best Buy and planted one of those recording devices instead."

"Well, fuckety fuck. I'd better schedule another sweep of our offices just in case."

She uttered the curse with such a brisk, no-nonsense air, he couldn't help bursting out in laughter. He caught the gleam of amusement in her eyes before her gaze seemed to change, stuck like a piece of gum on the bottom of a shoe, stubborn and clingy and refusing to budge.

She was staring at his bare chest.

His breath stilled. The air seemed to singe with heat and grow heavy between them. A sudden surge of awareness that had never been there before filled the space—or at least, one that had never been recognized. Her pale cheeks turned pink, and her lips parted slightly as if it were hard for her to draw in a breath. For endless seconds, he stood locked to the floor, afraid to move away from the shimmering heat in her gaze as it touched on his nakedness. Her perusal swept over his shoulders, moved down to his pecs, and settled at the line above his belt buckle. He felt himself grow hard from the visual caress and clenched his teeth as he struggled for control.

But, God, he wanted her to look up. Right at him. Deep into his eyes so he could finally see if there was something there that she was desperately fighting, too. Needed to know he wasn't alone in this sudden, crazed need for her.

She turned back around. Her voice never faltered. "Fifteen minutes left. By the way, the Make-A-Wish foundation fundraiser is this Friday."

He pushed away the disappointment that crashed through him at her obvious disinterest. He was nuts. She didn't feel anything toward him except a mild interest in his physique, a flickering appreciation from a female toward a male who took care of his body and stayed fit. Nothing more. Nothing less. He shrugged on his shirt and quickly buttoned it up. "You know I can't go. I have to show up and do my part for the damn political fundraiser for Devons."

"Devons sorely lacks political appeal," she recited primly.

"Devons is an idiot, and we all know it. But for now, he's my idiot, and better that than our combatant." He slid on his jacket and straightened his tie. "I'm forced to go and play nice for my party. Anyway, you said you'd go in my place to represent the office."

"And I will, but the Hope for Heroes organization is part of the fundraiser, dedicated to pediatric cancer research. Cameron's making an appearance. He's out of the hospital."

He stilled. Cameron was a six-year-old boy fighting leukemia who had always wanted to be a firefighter. Jonathan had met him in the hospital with the fire chief and worked with the foundation to give the boy a full day at the local firehouse, riding on the truck and joining the guys for a big homemade dinner the chief had cooked. The boy's fierce strength and smile, along with his mop of curly red hair, had charmed Jonathan from the first. He began visiting Cameron regularly, and when he started to hear about the low funding for childhood cancer compared to other causes, he got more involved. "How's he doing?"

One of Alyssa's rare smiles curved her lips. His chest tightened with the beauty of it. "Much better. He'll be saying a few words, though. I figured you should know in case you decide to change plans. Ten minutes left."

He groaned, torn. "I'll get my ass handed to me if I don't show, Alyssa. Especially now that I'm running for governor."

She lifted a brow. "I know. I'm not trying to talk you out of anything. Just giving you the full itinerary of information for you to make a final decision."

He glared. Re-dressed, he strode to his desk and skimmed through the newest agendas, ignoring the furiously blinking phone lines, his fat inbox, and the endless tasks he had to get through before he could call it a day. "There's no other decision to make. I can't back out on Devons. It'll look bad."

"Of course, I understand completely."

"I know you hate going to these things alone, but I need you to cover for me."

She nodded. "Done. One minute. Oh, and I'm not going alone."

He clenched his fingers around the file and stared at her. "What?"

She pivoted on her sensible heel and headed to the door. He heard her talk into the earpiece permanently attached to her ear. "They're waiting in the conference room."

"Alyssa."

Did he shout, or was his tone ridiculously high? It's just she never brought dates to these functions, not once since he'd known her. She'd told him over and over that work functions were for work, not pleasure. Had a man finally changed her mind?

Someone who wasn't him?

"Yes, Mr. Mayor?"

He practically gripped the edge of the desk in his need not to pounce across the room and begin flinging personal, inappropriate questions at her. "Do I know him? I mean, is he from the office, helping you out?"

She hesitated. He felt like a damn puppy, begging to know that she wasn't really attached. And for what? So he could declare his intentions to be the man she needed? The man to fuck her and protect her and care for her in the way he'd been fantasizing about?

If he hadn't been so focused on every nuance of her expression, he would have missed the regret flickering across her profile—the tightness of her lip, the determined set of her shoulders. Finally, she spoke, her voice a tad huskier than normal. "No. I have a date. But don't worry, I won't let it affect the job. Time's up."

She left.

Chapter Four

Alyssa worked her way through the elegant crowd, stopping to chat up various people, both those whom she knew and ones she hoped to know better. The event was being held at the New York City Library, a big, splashy party meant to draw out the best of the city's upper crust in order to help terminally ill children achieve their lifelong wishes.

Because, for most of them, life was too heartbreakingly short.

He should have been here.

Disappointment flickered through her even as she swatted it aside like a gnat. Jonathan was a strong advocate of Make-A-Wish and pediatric cancer research foundations, using his platform to raise awareness and to help. Since his wife had died of breast cancer, Alyssa had expected him to take up that specific cause, or rescue animals like his daughter. Although it seemed he tried to support as many important charities as possible, this was where his heart lay—along with helping the city's homeless.

She didn't know why, and maybe there were no solid reasons. Yet another mystery surrounding Jonathan Lake. Of course, she had no right to hope he'd change his plans when he needed to schmooze and secure as many power players as possible. Unfortunately, they'd both learned that equaled voters. Politics had many slimy underground tunnels hidden beneath polished smiles and endless promises, but she'd found there were good people too, usually caught in the web. The strong ones survived and kept their platform as pure as possible, yet mastered the art of compromise. Jonathan could have turned bitter, or even worse, apathetic.

Instead, the more obstacles he faced, the harder he seemed to fight for his ideals.

Another reason she'd begun to fall so hard for him.

Alyssa plucked a glass of champagne from a tray and glanced up at her escort. "Shall we make our way to the left or the right?"

Paul grinned. "Haven't you learned yet? You start in the middle."

She smiled back. She'd sat next to him at one of those boring recognition breakfasts and ended up enjoying his easy-going manner and humor. He was older but attractive, with sparkling brown eyes, salt and pepper hair, and a meaty, muscled body she appreciated. He'd been asking her out for a while now, but she'd always felt something more akin to friendship than attraction. Still, she needed to try. Especially after *the incident.*

She'd looked.

Broken her cardinal rule. *Never see him naked.* She was used to him changing clothes in a flash while she was in the office, but not once had she glimpsed even a shred of bare skin. They were ruthlessly careful to never cross the line, especially since neither of them appreciated office gossip. But this time, his laugh had charmed her like Medusa, and when she'd looked, she'd been turned to stone.

The memory of his glorious, chiseled chest on full display made a shudder wrack her body. The perfect dusting of dark, crisp hair trailing down in a magic line that disappeared under the belt of his pants. The bunch of biceps and strong line of a shoulder she ached to sink her teeth into. He'd stood before her, thighs braced apart, on full display, frozen in stillness as if he sensed the sudden surge of heat between them. The idea that he suspected she was hot for him made her cheeks burn. She'd done the only thing possible.

Pretended not to be affected and got back to business.

Shaking her head, she refocused. "The middle it is. I need to make sure I see Cam, and the director, and a few of the mayor's business associates. Are you sure you won't be bored? I feel like I'm still at work."

He waved his hand in the air. "It's fine. I need to do some networking myself. I'm just happy you finally accepted my invite."

She frowned. "Well, I technically invited you, but I'm glad, too."

He laughed and patted her arm. "You have a strange sense of humor. I like it."

Alyssa didn't take offense. She'd heard it way too often and had been called *Spock* by her own parents. She never understood jokes and sucked at sarcasm, instead, attacking her views on life in ways that made sense. She simply couldn't relate to many people and had made peace with it long ago.

Most she didn't like anyway.

Switching on her public façade, she pasted a smile on her face and attacked the throng. It was a good hour later that she was able to touch base with Cam. Dressed in a mini suit and tie, his bald head only accentuated his Irish blue eyes full of a zest for life she wished the world had more of. She hugged his parents hello where they flanked him, then knelt down in front of the guest of honor.

"Hi, Cam. You look extremely handsome tonight. How are you feeling?"

"Today's a good day." His smile was all sweetness, and her heart squeezed with both pain and happiness. He'd been through so much already, and they were praying this latest round of chemo had kicked him back into remission. "Is Jonathan here?"

She shook her head. "I'm sorry, sweetie, he couldn't come. He had a really important meeting, but he sent me. Told me to tell you he'll call you later and he's proud of you."

He seemed to process the words. "Okay. Did you know the chief got me a real fireman's jacket?"

She smiled with relief, knowing at six years old, he was easily distracted. Good. He'd bonded with Jonathan, but there was enough excitement here to keep him from feeling the mayor's lack of presence. "That's really cool. You should have worn it with your suit."

His laugh said it was funny, even though she hadn't meant it as a joke. Many people in the crowd wore gear to support Make-A-Wish and various cancer research funds. Cam looked up and, suddenly his face brightened. "Alyssa, the meeting is over!"

"What meeting?"

"The one Jonathan was at!" He began waving his hand in the air. She frowned, not understanding.

"Hey, champ. Well, don't you look like Bruce Wayne today. Not planning to fight the Joker tonight, are you?"

The familiar, gravelly voice hit her straight in the solar plexus. She straightened, her heart beating madly against her ribcage like a bird whose flight couldn't be contained. *He's here.* She tried to pull it together, but she'd discovered that she did better when she prepped herself for his presence. She sucked at surprises.

Jonathan tousled the kid's hair and beamed down. Cam puffed up. "Jonathan, I got a real red fireman's jacket!"

"No way. How am I supposed to top what Chief gave you?" He scratched his head and tried to consider. "Don't think I can, but at least I have this cool shirt."

Cam stared at his fancy, long, wool coat, currently covering Jonathan up. "What shirt?"

He winked. "This one." He unbuttoned his coat and flashed it open. Cam's eyes widened, and he giggled, tugging at his father's sleeve.

Alyssa saw the black T-shirt with the bright red logo *F--- Cancer* scrawled across the front. Paired with his fancy pants and dress shoes, he should have looked ridiculous. Instead, he looked cool. He shrugged off his outerwear and gave Cam's parents high-fives. A murmur rose from the people surrounding him, and Alyssa caught the gentling of faces as they gazed at the current mayor and Cam together.

Bulbs flashed. It was a great moment meant for viewing and to increase votes. The thing was, Alyssa knew for a fact that Jonathan hadn't done any of it for attention or the election. He'd been quietly visiting and supporting Cam and the family, along with dozens of other families he'd become close to during his research into childhood cancer. But she knew people would judge anyway, calling him out for making himself seem sympathetic to a hot cause when he'd just announced his run for governor.

Alyssa's mind went over Jonathan's mantra that he consistently repeated.

It's not my business what other people think of me, but in this job, I have to at least be aware.

Balance was key. Already, he'd quietly buttoned his suit jacket back up over the shirt, handing his wool coat to his bodyguard, who pawned it off to his general assistant. He chatted with Cam's parents for a while, gave the boy a pep talk regarding the sentences he'd practiced to utter into the microphone, then turned toward her.

His warm smile had faded, replaced by his business persona—a mix of professional yet friendly he consistently showed the world. She was used to it, but she couldn't help it when her gaze probed, dove deep into piercing, ocean-blue eyes, and faltered.

A flash of sizzling heat zinged back at her.

"Where's your date?" he asked.

She blinked. "Around. Why are you here?"

His shoulders lifted slightly. "Did my required time and made my appearance. Decided this was too important to miss." His gaze narrowed. "This guy isn't worth your time."

Fascinated, she leaned a few inches forward. "Why?"

His jaw clenched. "Because he left you alone for too long. He should know better, Alyssa."

"Mr. Mayor!" a voice rang out.

In a flash, Jonathan's smile was back, his gaze once again guarded. "I need to speak to you after the party." Then he was gone, swallowed up by the crowds. Her mouth fell half-open like a guppy, and a terrible, aching emptiness flooded her insides as if just the nearness of his body heat had filled her from within.

What the hell just happened?

She had no time to process because Paul materialized by her side. "Okay, networking done. You still officially on the clock, or can you take a break?"

Jonathan's words still echoed in her ears. The sexy, almost commanding comment made her toes curl in her sensible shoes. Desperate to finally feel something with anyone but her boss, she determinedly linked her arm through Paul's and forced a smile. "Yes, let's take a walk and get a drink. I need a breather."

He seemed pleased as he guided her across the room. The tall columns and stacks of books surrounding her bore silent witness to the lie she was already beginning to form. That maybe Paul would be the guy to get her to stop thinking about the mayor.

She hoped. But, unfortunately, she knew the answer already.

* * * *

The guy was no threat.

At least, not yet.

Jonathan recognized his arrogant thought without flinching and realized that the relief unfurling in his gut was a sign. He'd watched them throughout the evening with eagle-eyed precision, searching for any intimate gestures. Oh, she'd touched the guy many times, causing a primitive surge of testosterone to rear its ugly head inside him, but there wasn't even a hint of chemistry between the two. She hadn't tipped up her head and treated him to that half-smile she flashed when she became amused. There was no adorable frown between her brows when she spoke, which told Jonathan that she wasn't challenged by any of their conversations. She didn't lean in when they stood side by side, and seemed more interested in doing her job than trying to build a connection.

The knowledge that he still hadn't lost her shattered the last of his control. These past weeks, he'd been desperately fighting his growing need for more. The look on her face when she'd stared at him half-undressed hinted at a deeper attraction and emotion he'd never dreamt of. Was it possible she was just as good as he was at hiding her true feelings? They'd spent multiple late nights alone together. Constantly worked side by side. But he'd been ruthless about keeping any type of personal relationship separate. Dear God, in a way, he knew nothing about her. Not her parents or upbringing. Not her hopes and dreams or even if she had any. She kept herself locked behind a wall, refusing to give him anything. And for the past two years, it'd been exactly what he wanted.

Until now.

Every voice in his head screamed at him to back off. He'd been so careful to keep himself in check and avoid any type of romantic entanglements at work. Nothing good could come of opening Pandora's Box. Even if they both copped to having an attraction, the pitfalls of this type of relationship were not merely stumbling blocks. They were complete dead-ends.

Yet...

He ached to try. If she rejected his advances, he'd leave her alone. He'd had enough practice locking up his emotions over the years, and he'd never put her in an uncomfortable position. He respected her way too much for that bullshit.

Since Catherine had died, no women had stirred his desire. He'd refused to date, happy to settle in to his full-time lover—work. But Alyssa was different. His interest and emotions had grown steadily, until one day, it felt as if he'd been moving toward her the entire time. He just hadn't been prepared for it.

She appeared at the top of the stairs. Her cocktail dress was conservative and black, a polished number that screamed respectable yet elegant, the hem past the knee. There were no fuck-me shoes, just plain leather pumps with a low heel. Her hair remained up in a tight bun, but it only emphasized the softness of her features—the gentle curve of her cheek, the stubborn chin, and those pursed lips that gleamed wetly from her rose-colored gloss. He loved that she changed for nobody and didn't seem interested in the normal trappings of the female persuasion. God knew she didn't need any help being the sexiest woman in the room. Her brain was the biggest turn-on of all.

A wispy longing rose up inside him. He ached to have the right to touch her. To slide his fingers into hers, yank, and have her soft body collapse against his chest. He imagined unpinning the knot from her hair and burying his hands in the silky blond strands. Burned to experience the imprint of her full lips under his, opening to the thrust of his tongue, hips arched and begging for a release she wanted only from—

"Mr. Mayor?" She tipped her head and treated him to an appraising stare behind her tortoiseshell glasses. "You needed to see me?"

He swallowed past the sudden knot in his throat and shot his cuffs. "Yes. I realize it's late, but I had some concerns regarding the latest budget expenditures. I'm out of the office tomorrow. Do you have an hour to go over it?"

She paused. He could practically hear her brain clicking madly over the spreadsheets she'd probably memorized. Her skill with accounting and budgets had made him weep with pure relief. "Yes. But I thought it'd been finalized."

"So did I, but I spoke with some board members at Devons' function, and there was pushback on some of the funding. I need to re-allocate."

She nodded. "Of course. I already said good-bye to Paul. Let's go."

He escorted her into the back of the car. The clean scent of cotton filled his nostrils, both comforting and arousing. Her dress hitched a few inches higher, revealing a smooth, bare knee. No stockings. He imagined what type of panties she wore. Fantasized about sliding his hand under that very proper fabric and discovering—

He jerked himself out of the daydream and cleared his throat. "Did you enjoy the party?"

"Yes."

He tried not to smile at her brief answers. She rarely elaborated, and he liked to push at certain subjects, deciding what he wanted more detail on. The dynamic worked well for them. "Cam did well."

"I'm glad you came. Seeing you makes him happy. And the shirt was a big hit."

He winced. "Didn't realize I'd have a camera crew following me around. I'll probably get hit with another round of people accusing me of mugging for election publicity."

She gave an elegant shrug. "You didn't do it for that purpose. At this point, you need to be clear on what you're doing for PR and for yourself. As long as you know the difference, it will be fine."

He shook his head. "Who taught you to be so diplomatic? You've always been able to cut through the bullshit and see things most don't. Are your parents just as sharp?"

She gazed at him with a touch of surprise. He realized it was the first real personal question he'd asked her since Paul. Two in one night. No wonder she was off-kilter. She answered slowly as if picking her words carefully. "Smart, yes. But nothing like me. They're much more…colorful."

He wanted to ask more, but they'd reached his townhouse. She peered out the window. "Wait, I thought we were going to the office."

He watched her closely. "My home is closer, and I have all the files on my laptop. But if you feel more comfortable, I can have Tim drive us to City Hall."

His palms started to sweat like a teen while he analyzed the emotions that flickered over her face. If he sensed real discomfort, he was ready to turn the car back around. He wanted her in his home, surrounded by his personal things so he could begin chipping away at the barrier between them. But the wall had to come down because they both wanted it.

"No, I'm good," she said.

He relaxed. "Thank you, Tim. If you can, please wait for when Alyssa needs to be driven home."

"Of course, sir. Have a good night."

They made their way into the brownstone where he'd resided for the past few years. He'd moved out of his last place after Catherine passed and settled in for the past five years as first the DA, and then the mayor. It had the hushed elegance of old money and was situated on a prominent street, but the inside wasn't pretentious. Instead, it was decorated with a modern simplicity he liked, especially as a single man.

Alyssa had been to his house many times, but usually only to drop off files or share in a brief discussion amidst frantic appointments. Tonight, there was a deeper quiet that permeated the space as he walked to the kitchen, shedding his jacket and flipping it over the espresso leather sectional. "I'll bring out my laptop, take a seat," he called out, letting her take a moment to settle. "Can I get you a drink? I have a nice cabernet open."

"Sure."

He grabbed two glasses and filled them a quarter full, then pulled out some chunk cheese, Triscuits, and grapes. Arranging everything onto a plate, he carried out the snack and set it on the glass table where he ate most of his meals while he worked. "I know you're starving," he said with a smile. "No one ever gets enough to eat at those fancy functions. Help yourself."

"Thanks."

She picked up the wine and swirled the glass absently before taking a deep sniff. "Are you a wine connoisseur?" he asked curiously.

"No. But you really taste the wine with your nose first. And the swirling of the glass means nothing. I just do it because it's fun."

He cocked his head. "I thought it tested the legs."

"The legs don't tell you if a wine is good or not. It just tells you if it has a high amount of alcohol. If you cover the glass, the legs disappear. See." She demonstrated. "Just a weird fact."

"Interesting." He retrieved his laptop, then sat down in one of the leather dining seats that matched his sectional. "So, we got interrupted. Why do you believe your parents are more colorful than you?"

Her fingers jerked over the cracker, telling him she was surprised he'd continued with their conversation. He watched her stack a cube of cheese on top, then pluck a grape from the bunch. She placed them into her mouth with precision. She attacked every activity with a slow, deliberate purpose that drove some people nuts, but completely turned him on.

"They're both actors," she finally said after chewing and swallowing. "Colorful is a kind word to describe them. Let's just say they believe the world is a stage, and live their lives that way."

Shock hit him. He would've imagined she'd grown up in a household of accountants, computer techs, or teachers. He leaned in, fascinated. "How was it living with them?"

A small noise left her throat. Sort of a ladylike snort. "Complicated. We traveled a lot—they were known to take jobs all over the world—so there was little stability. They believed in expressing their opinions loudly, and our house of the moment was always filled with starving artists with no money and many good intentions." Shadows fell across her face, but she avoided his gaze so he couldn't tell how she really felt. "They were never boring."

Her carefully phrased statements about her parents told him what he needed. "It must've been very hard to be so different," he said softly.

"Sometimes. We didn't understand each other, but I know they tried. I only wanted my books, my computer, and my private space. I loved school and libraries and did my best to stay away from the chaos of the theater. They hated institutions that provided, as they said, robotic thoughts and a narrow view on society, so they used to keep me away from school a lot. Said I'd get a real education experiencing life. I used to think I was adopted."

He raised a brow. "Were you?"

"No. All children spin that fantasy when they don't get along with their parents. I was no different." She took another cracker, made a duplicate mini sandwich, and popped it into her mouth.

"When I was mad at my parents, I used to pray I'd get really sick," he said. "I planned to end up in the hospital—near death, of course—so they'd beg for my forgiveness. Then I'd get anything I wanted for the rest of my life because they were so grateful I survived."

There it was.

Her lips curved, and he caught the light pop in her big, brown eyes. "Another popular childhood fantasy."

"Did you have any siblings?" he asked.

She shook her head. "Just me and endless aunts and uncles of the theater."

"When did you finally get to pursue your own dream of college?"

"I left them when I was nineteen. Took my GED, applied to the local community college, and got a job working as a secretary. I taught myself to type and did the bills at home and for the current theater project they were involved in, so I had some skills. The rest was easy."

She sipped at the wine, taking her time with the balance and flavor as she let it settle over her tongue and slip down her throat. He shifted in the chair, the heat suddenly strangling him. She was so damn sexy and had no clue. It made it so much harder not to touch her.

"How easy?" he asked.

"I got As, scored a scholarship to Cornell, then came to the city for a more interesting career."

"Do you see your parents often?"

He wondered when she'd stop answering his questions. He was greedy for anything she'd share, but for now, she seemed open to talking. "No, but we chat on the phone, and when they came here last year for an off-off-Broadway play, they stayed with me for a week. We're happier when we're apart. Our personalities just never matched, but we love each other. We're family."

Her simple acceptance of her life humbled him. He knew she was no whiner, but it was more than that. She seemed to know who she was to the core and made no apologies—even to her parents. That type of strength and feminine confidence pulled at him. The man she took into her inner circle would be the luckiest bastard on Earth.

God, he wanted it to be him.

"Thank you for telling me," he finally said, content to let what she gave him be enough. "I guess I realized we spend all this time together, but I knew nothing about your personal life." Had he seemed greedy for information? Maybe it was better to ease off in case she was uncomfortable? "It's nice to learn more about your important employees."

She stiffened, and the wall slammed back up. "Our work relationship doesn't warrant personal," she said coolly. "And I don't need to be another of your charities, Mr. Mayor. The way things have been between us has been just fine."

He blinked, caught off guard. "Wait, what did I say wrong? And you know it pisses me off when you don't use my name."

Her chin tilted up, and she gave him a cutting glare over the frame of her glasses. "Excuse me if I'm suspicious regarding your sudden interest in me. Are you concerned I won't stick with you when you move on to governor? Are you experiencing guilt that you don't know your team well enough to count on their loyalty? Forgive me if I don't feel like being your first experiment in the heart-to-heart sharing segment. We should move on now."

His head spun. Oh, he'd pegged this all wrong. He'd wanted to give her space, but now she believed his interest in her was only to strengthen their bond from a work standpoint. Apparently, she had no clue his motivations were strictly personal. That he wanted to get to know her as a woman—not his assistant. He shouldn't have used the term *employee*.

He hesitated, not sure how much to give her before she spooked. "Alyssa, I'm sorry if that came out wrong. My questions had nothing to do with work, or the election, or making you feel happier in your job. I simply want to know you better."

She stared at him, and the air grew thick between them. "Why?"

Her direct question deserved a candid answer. "Because I really like you. More than you know."

He wanted to duck his head like a schoolboy to avoid her reaction, but he forced himself to hold her gaze and take the hit. Her pupils dilated, and a flush crept up her neck, flooding her cheeks. He wasn't surprised at the slight shock as she retreated—he'd been expecting it. No, he dreaded the distaste or embarrassment or panic that might occur, and he swore to back off if he caught any of it.

Instead, he watched the blush deepen, and her lips part, and the slam of a fierce hunger glint from behind those glasses. Her fingers trembled slightly as she reached for her wine and took a long swig, past caring about delicacy.

That's when he realized she wanted him, too.

His heart slammed hard and fast like a contractor with a jackhammer. The rush of relief was paired with the knowledge that she might turn away from him anyway. Hell, she was probably smart to get up, leave his place, and slam the door behind her, choosing to ignore his comment.

She set the glass down and dared to look at him. "I see."

He waited for more, but she seemed to be done. He fought a smile. Typical. He had women falling all over him every day, but Alyssa could care less. "I don't want to make you uncomfortable. You have every right to stop this conversation from going further, and I won't mention it again."

That adorable frown resurfaced. "I know that."

"Good. What do you think?"

"I think this is a dangerous conversation." She gave a tiny sigh. "I think you've always been clear about what you want in the office, and that's no entanglements."

"You're right. But after spending two years with you? I've changed my mind," he said simply.

She shook her head. "Tonight. Because you saw me with a date. Right?"

He didn't like where she was going with this. "Well, yes."

"I've seen plenty of RomComs, Jonathan. Working assistant is ignored by her boss. She shows up with a hot guy at a party, then boss gets a lightbulb moment he may have made a mistake by disregarding her as a woman, so he begins pursuit, convinced she was always *the one*. Textbook. I'm sure if you sleep on it, you'll change your mind in the morning and realize we should remain status quo."

He stared at her, torn between laughter and frustration. "You think I'm following a romantic comedy? Alyssa, I've been thinking of you in more ways than as my assistant for a while now. I just didn't want to push in case you weren't interested. I didn't want you to feel awkward or pressured and ruin the best thing I've ever had."

"Exactly. The best assistant you've ever had. You're blurring the lines because you realized another man may take me away, and you're worried about our working relationship. I should have brought a date to these functions long ago. Then you would've been able to move past the block and have more time to process."

He rubbed his head. "I don't think you're giving either of us enough credit. I know it's a risk. But would you be willing to try and get to know one another outside the workplace? See if this connection has legs?"

That tiny flicker of humor he spotted made him sure he'd be good for her. He loved every conversation he engaged in with her, challenged to keep his brain sharp enough to be a worthy partner. "May I ask if you and Paul are serious?"

He already knew the answer, but he wanted to see how she'd react.

"No, we're better as friends."

"That's what I thought. Alyssa, it's been a long time since I've been interested in a woman. I don't take this lightly—my emotions or my career."

Her voice softened. "I know. But you can't expect me to just announce I'd like to date you, and suddenly we're in the office together, and I'm confused about how to act. It'd be disastrous for both of us."

"I agree. I said I liked you. Not that I want to ravish you on my desk every day at three p.m."

She pursed her lips in disapproval. "Desk sex would be a nightmare. It'd take hours to get you reorganized."

His laugh came out too loud, clearly startling her, but then she smiled, acknowledging his reaction. "See? That's why I can't get you off my mind. I love your brain."

She blinked, and a flash of pleasure lit her pretty brown eyes. He bet she wasn't used to compliments from men. She deserved to be told how special she was every damn day. He hoped he got the chance.

"Then what are you proposing?" she asked.

"Just dinner. Alone. An opportunity to talk outside the office and chill. How does that sound?"

"I don't know," she finally said. "I'd still rather you sleep on it and decide later. Your primitive male self doesn't need to be threatened by me replacing you with someone else right now. Let's just say there's no other man in my life, and I'm sure it will continue that way."

He hated the tinge of sadness in her voice, the touch of loneliness she desperately tried to hide. He recognized it because he battled it every day and every night and still hadn't been able to make peace with his solitary existence the way he'd hoped. "If that will make you feel better, why don't we both think about it. We'll set dinner for Thursday night, and if either of us changes our mind, we'll never mention this again. Deal?"

He had to offer her an escape clause. It was the right thing, even though the idea of her running away broke something inside him. Slowly, she nodded. "Deal. Except you have the school board hearing on Thursday."

"Friday."

"You're meeting with the governor and then attending the senator's fundraiser."

"Saturday. And if you come up with something else I'm supposed to be doing, cancel it."

She wrinkled her nose. "We could do it late, around nine p.m. That's all you can manage. I double-booked you."

"I'll take it."

Negotiating with his schedule for a dinner date was ridiculous, but there was no other woman who could make it seem so damn sexy. Her clean scent hit his nostrils and made him dizzy.

"I should look at those spreadsheets," she said a bit shyly, shifting in her seat.

He realized he'd pushed enough and needed to back off and let her breathe. "Of course."

He brought up the necessary Excel files, turning the laptop around so they could both see the screen. "I spoke with the senator tonight, and he mentioned there may be too many funds earmarked for the Back to Home program."

She dragged her chair a few inches closer so she could view the laptop. He studied her as she morphed into work-mode, her nose pinched beneath her glasses as her gaze flickered across the screen, taking in the endless columns of figures. "That program is your baby," she said shortly. "We're at the minimum budget to run it properly."

"I agree. But I'm still getting pushback, and we're low on funding for the libraries at this point."

"But stats on the homeless this quarter were way down. We need all those funds to keep the program successful."

"Tell that to the librarians who need to keep up with technology. They need a computer system upgrade, and it's going to cost. It'll be on Harry's desk to work his magic, but I wanted your opinion first."

Budgets were thorny, and it'd only get worse when he got bumped to governor. Running a state was more complicated than running a city, but he felt up to the task and had decent skills in the art of compromise. Too bad other politicians didn't. God knew it would make the country a better place if they did. "I'll have to cut a layer of cost somehow, but I don't want to backtrack at this point."

Her glossy, naked nail tapped against her lip, and then she reached for his keyboard, clicking madly through the tabs and programs as if seeing something he didn't. "You can't cut shelter security," she murmured, "or the foundation will crumble. But we earmarked for a ton of admin. If we don't hire those two new positions and switch them to volunteers, we may be able to handle the squeeze."

"Mary said those positions were needed."

"They are, but if we switch them to give college credit as an internship instead of pay, it could still work."

He leaned back, considering. Once again, she was able to move boxes around and see a different picture. It was a talent he relied on every day in order to do the best job possible. There was no way he could lose her.

Damnit.

He studied the nape of her neck, the vulnerable, smooth flesh practically begging for his lips. He wondered what would happen if he leaned forward and pressed his mouth there or ran his tongue slowly down the length of her spine, relishing every shudder and shiver. But if he made a move too soon, before she was ready, he might lose her completely. "An internship may not give Mary what she needs."

"It's a competitive market. I'm sure we can vet the correct volunteers who want to do a kick-ass job and impress the mayoral office."

She was right. The odds were in their favor. "That's a brilliant idea, Alyssa. Thank you."

"You're welcome. I'm sure Harry would've come up with the same solution."

Jonathan doubted it, but he was used to her aversion to gushing compliments on the job.

A short silence settled between them, filled with all the things spoken and unspoken over the past hour. He was about to tell her how much he admired her, that she was the type of woman deserving of a man who was worthy. That he was honored she'd chosen to accompany him for dinner. But she quickly stood up and made her announcement. "I should be going."

He scrambled back, feeling overly awkward and not at all like a man who ran one of the most powerful cities in the US. "Yes, of course. Thanks again for helping me out. Tim will get you home safe."

She nodded, buttoned up her coat, and headed for the door.

"Alyssa?"

Her hand stilled on the knob. Sensual tension cranked between them. "Yes?"

"Make sure you come in late tomorrow morning. Ten a.m., no earlier. I kept you out too late tonight for work. Okay?"

He heard her draw in a deep breath. "Okay."

Then she was gone.

Chapter Five

Dinner with the mayor.

Her boss.

Her secret crush.

This was insanity.

The thoughts whirled in her head with every step through the hallway, snapping automatically into work-mode. She'd come in at 9:30 a.m. the next morning, expecting him to explain he'd had too much to drink and had decided it was best for both of them to keep their relationship platonic.

Instead, he'd scolded her for the half-hour, snapped into mayoral-mode, and later on, she'd found their dinner date on his calendar marked in bold.

Guess he was still serious. And today was D-day. She'd spent a ridiculous amount of time wondering what she should wear before deciding on her work clothes since they'd probably leave straight from the office. Not that she had any sexy date clothes, anyway. They were all black, conservative, classic. And boring.

Oh, well. She liked them, and one date didn't warrant her tossing out her stuff in order to match his type. Alyssa knew well the women Jonathan tended to date. His late wife fit the standard: dynamic, passionate, and beautiful. The media loved to attach him to numerous women and speculate on romantic trysts—he was pretty much the darling of reporters and gossip rags. Even more so because he'd been so careful not to get involved with anyone, though actresses, models, and lawyers desperately tried. He'd actually been linked to a famous tennis star who killed it at Wimbledon.

But they all fizzled out into friendships then faded to nothing.

Yet, here she was, ready to go on a date he'd asked for. Her belly swam with fluttering butterflies, especially when she remembered the way he'd uttered those amazing words, his ocean-blue eyes locked on hers.

I like you, Alyssa. I like you a lot.

Shakespeare could do no better.

The hours flew by, crammed with endless meetings, mini-disasters, and the frenzy that came with dealing with the public. Slowly, people left to run home to families or dates or commitments, and she found herself alone at her desk, working on some email responses. It was almost nine p.m. when Jonathan finally strode out, saying goodbye to the small team of suits that advised him in various facets.

Her palms sweated as he leaned over. The ocean scent of his cologne always hit her hard, a precursor to the powerful male energy that swarmed around her. His thick, dark hair looked mussed, and lines of weariness bracketed his eyes. She noticed his red tie a bit askew, and the top button of his crisp, white shirt loosened. Yep, his meeting with the educators had not gone well. "I'm sorry I'm late," he said in a low voice. His gaze flicked over her work clothes. "Do you need to go home and change first?"

She fought the trickle of doubt at her appearance, deciding he'd better learn early on that she didn't intend to dazzle with her wardrobe or makeup skills. Her black, raw silk jacket, pants, and tank were standard fare. "No. But are you sure you want to go? You look tired. We can cancel."

His jaw firmed, but his eyes gentled as he smiled. "It was the only thing I was looking forward to all day," he said simply. "Thank you for waiting. Tim's out front."

Alyssa hesitated. Her inner voice screamed that this was her chance to back out of the whole thing, but her feet automatically moved as she locked up her desk and followed him out. His hand guided her from the small of her back, and the intimate gesture made goosebumps prickle over her skin. They'd walked down the hallways hundreds of times before, but this time, she felt like a woman.

Not his assistant.

"Where are we going?" she asked, settling into the comfortable back seat.

"Italian good? I'm craving some comfort food."

"Sure. I just think it would be best if the restaurant wasn't..." She trailed off, not yet comfortable expressing how she felt about the evening.

"Close?" She nodded slowly. "I understand, Alyssa. I figured *Felice* has good food, but it's not too far out of the way, and no one should bother us there."

"Thanks." Silence settled around them, but she felt no pressure to make casual conversation. She looked out the window and watched the city whiz by, the roads emptier at the later hour. Trying to get anywhere during rush hour in Manhattan was impossible, and they'd both rather walk if possible, rather than sit in a car for an hour not moving. "I'm sorry Andrew gave you a hard time with the push to stifle vaping."

He stared at her in surprise. "How did you know? I hoped our inability to agree was kept quiet for now until I get more support on the proposal. Did you see the new health report? Too many kids still think it's not like smoking a cigarette."

She rolled her eyes. "Jonathan, he's pissed off you're going for governor. He'll do his best to stifle you on every idea you have until you win the election. Don't tell me you didn't realize."

He tilted his head as if analyzing her words. "I knew he was temperamental, but I figured we'd gotten past that hump. He backed me on the limitations for soda in the vending machines."

"Only because Henderson wanted it. Not you."

"Son of a bitch," he whispered under his breath. "I think you're right."

"You should mention it during the Healthy New York run next week. Get it more on your radar."

"I will. I'm going to make sure we have better awareness programs in the schools, too." He paused, and she felt his gaze boring into her. "How was your day?"

"Productive." She rattled off everything she'd accomplished like a well-oiled machine. "Tomorrow, I think I want to change your agenda for the—"

"Alyssa."

Her name was a command and a question, spoken in that low, silky voice that caressed her nerve endings. She fought a shiver. "Yes?"

"I didn't mean work. I meant how you were feeling. I'd like to say we're officially off the clock and out of the office. What did you have for lunch? Did you sleep well? Anything interesting happen?"

A rare smile tugged at her lips. His inquiries were sweet. When was the last time anyone had asked her any boring questions about her day? Certainly, never her parents. She had no other family. And her friends were all co-workers, where she'd occasionally meet for a drink at the bar and listen to them bitch about work and target the single men. She ended up going home early while they stayed to party and hook up. She never really felt like she fit in with any group, so she'd decided she didn't need one at all. She refused to apologize for being a misfit. It suited her.

"Well, I read the new Malcolm Gladwell book for an hour, then used this lotion that's supposed to encourage a deeper REM sleep, which will end up giving me more energy for less sleep if it works out. Smells a bit funky, and it's purple, but I'll give it a thirty-day trial run." She glanced at him to check his boredom level, but he was looking at her with an eagerness she didn't think he could fake. Might as well finish. "I had a Caesar salad at my desk with a green smoothie, so I'd say my free radicals are burning up nicely, and I did a quick walk over in the park to get to my ten thousand steps." Health was important to her. The body was a machine, and she made sure to take care of it so it provided her with the fuel needed to function and flourish. "That's about it."

Ugh, she'd rambled again, but honestly, this was her life. He might as well realize she wasn't suddenly going to become more exciting just because she was dating him. She squared her shoulders, already defensive, but he nodded with interest. "Does the cream have lavender in it? I heard that's very soothing."

"Yes. Lavender, almond oil, cocoa butter, and oatmeal."

"Let me know if it works. I've tried melatonin and some nerve tonic, and nothing's done it for me."

"You have insomnia?"

His lips quirked. "I have public figure persona. It means I never sleep an entire night without waking up to stare at the ceiling and go over the million ways I can fail."

She tilted her head. "What about the million ways you make a difference?"

"I'm only on number three, so I have more work in that category."

A sigh escaped. "You're always too hard on yourself."

"That's my job, too. Making sure no one else has to police me," he said.

"Another reason I wanted to work with you. It's more than a job being your assistant. It's…fulfilling."

He stared at her, his gaze delving deep, an intent light in those ocean depths. "That's probably the highest compliment you've given me. But I wonder if you know how much you've done, not only for the office but also for me. I don't even think of you as an assistant. You're more like my partner."

She jerked slightly, his words slamming through her like a sucker punch. *Partner?* The intimate word stretched and settled between them, sparking the silence, but before she could analyze how she felt, the car pulled up to the curb.

The restaurant was low-key and intimate, and they were swept in and seated toward the back. One bodyguard stood discreetly away at a distance, but close enough to deal with any trouble. The owner came out to fuss, and after ordering some wine, they both agreed to order a few plates and share so they could taste a variety.

It dawned on her how much he really did know about her. Her likes and dislikes. Her hatred of iced tea and coffee and how she preferred both in heated form. Her secret love of dark chocolate and how she ate exactly one Dove bar per day, kept locked in the right-hand drawer of her desk. And he knew they both adored anything Italian, choosing to order in penne ala vodka and chicken parm on some awful, draining days, not caring about carbs or diet or that there wasn't a salad in sight.

She shook off her thoughts. Whatever they were doing here together—whether this was a real date or they were just figuring out if they were brave enough to try—it was a precious opportunity to know him more after the doors had closed. She wasn't about to waste it, so she dove in hard, not afraid to swim in the deep waters.

"When was your last relationship?" she asked. She might know the basics from an outsider's perspective, but she wanted the details and truth only he could give her.

He buttered a piece of bread, completely poised. "You mean sexually? Or romantically?"

His blunt question pleased her. She refused to blush, liking the way he wasn't afraid to tell the truth. "Both."

He slowly chewed a bite of bread and swallowed before answering. "My wife, romantically. Five years ago. As for sexually, I've had three extremely short weekend flings. I made sure I was upfront about my limitations, and they accepted what I couldn't give. I guess it's been a long time since dialogue with a woman stimulated me as much as a kiss."

She lifted a brow. "I'm surprised our conversations were memorable enough since we haven't kissed yet."

"Ah, but that word is all I need for stimulation."

"What word?"

He leaned over and whispered in his dark, sexy voice, "Yet."

She shook her head at his naughty humor and sipped her wine. "Three encounters aren't much over five years," she said thoughtfully.

He winced. "Yeah, let's just say no one knows about my low number, especially the press. The state wants me to be both celibate yet exciting like Clooney. It's an odd balance to keep, so I began taking dates to various functions but keeping things platonic. It's been easy to focus on work. It's all I ever needed, other than Chloe."

She thought over all the women she'd watched him take to splashy, glamorous events. How many nights she'd forced herself not to think of him taking them to bed, giving them the right to touch and taste and kiss him. How she'd pleasured herself in the dark with his face in her memory, imagining that she was enough to enthrall him. "Yet, here we are."

The words popped out before she could stop them, but she refused to cower. This was too important to tiptoe around what they were doing. Or not doing. Or thinking of doing. She needed to know the rules and what he expected after this date.

He locked his gaze on hers. Her breath caught as she tumbled into a flood of piercing, startling blue. "My favorite word again. Let me ask you this, Alyssa. When was your last relationship? Both romantic and sexual."

The waiter glided by, dropped off a few platters, then silently retreated. She helped herself to a generous bowl of shrimp capellini doused in fresh parmesan. "Romantically? A decade ago, in college. We dated for a year when he was a senior, but then he took off to California for sunshine and bigger opportunities. It was my first broken heart because it was the first time I'd stayed around somewhere long enough to fall in love. Sexually, I'm also a bit of a disappointment. I've only had a few brief affairs that ended quite pleasantly."

He frowned. "Somehow, I don't think the word *pleasant* should be used with the term affair."

She sighed. "Exactly. That's why they fizzled out. No true passion. Plus, I'm like you. I prefer work, and at home, I love my books and solitude. There's been little time for play."

"I love books, too. And I'm in the public eye so much, solitude is a slice of heaven." He cocked his head. "So we're both celibate and nerds."

"Guess so." The random fact floated in her head. "Did you know if a female ferret doesn't have sex for a year, she can die?"

He sat back in the seat and grinned at her. "Nope. But I don't think I'll ever forget it now. And I'm glad we're not ferrets."

She winced. "Sorry, I tend to do that. Too much info sometimes."

"I like it. Your big old brain is sexy as hell."

Startled, she looked up from her plate, but he was busy eating, looking as focused on the food in front of him as he was with his team in closed-door meetings. Which probably meant he brought the same intensity into the bedroom.

The thought stalled her out, but he was still speaking, so she refocused.

"I'm glad you found me interesting enough to come to dinner. I bet there aren't many men out there you'd find worthy," he said.

She blinked. "Oh, I've found interesting before, but never with someone like you."

"Like me how?"

"Hot."

He laughed with delight, and she almost rolled her eyes at her awful habit of blurting out anything in her head. And then he slid his hand across the table and enfolded her fingers with his. The shocking heat of his skin on hers made her belly clench, and a primal need roared through her blood. She returned the pressure, and then they were holding hands, staring at each other in the flickering candlelight.

"If we're gonna talk hot, you should know I've been having some wicked fantasies myself."

She scoffed. "I highly doubt it. I'm the first one to admit there's not an ounce of sexpot within me."

His eyes darkened, and his fingers tightened over hers. "Oh, if you only knew, Alyssa," he said softly. "The hot librarian image is a cliché for a reason. And when you start rattling off statistics like a master, I get a bit weak-kneed."

A laugh burst from her lips. "You're insane."

"God, I love when you do that."

"What?"

A flicker of tenderness skated over his features. "Smile. Laugh. It's like the sun coming out on a cloudy day."

It was a ridiculous and awful compliment with no originality, but it was his expression and the honest way he said it that got her. Jonathan didn't take the time to sputter inanities at women.

So if he said it, he meant it.

Her head spun with a heady lightness that made her feel as if she'd drunk a bottle of wine. She sucked at flirting.

But something told her that's what they were doing, and quite successfully. She didn't feel awkward around him like she'd worried about. It was as if their relationship had just flowed from the office to private without a hitch.

"Mr. Mayor! What a lovely surprise!"

The feminine voice made Alyssa yank her hand back, making her look even more suspiciously guilty. She watched as Jonathan's face shut down and morphed into politician mask. He leaned back in his seat as if to create as much distance as possible between them. "Whitney, how are you? What brings you out at this late hour?"

Whitney Burke, charity organizer extraordinaire, Upper East Side aristocrat with blood that flowed as blue as a summer sky, trained her razor-sharp gaze on them. It was as if she scented scandal and thrived on the aroma. Personally, Alyssa had never had a problem with her because she never held any surprises. She wanted money for her various foundations, craved attention from the press and handsome men, and wanted to re-marry for status, not love. A tall, willowy brunette who reminded Alyssa of Snow White, she was both stunning and a touch cold. She'd been linked to Jonathan many times, probably by her own leaked gossip, and papers still thrilled at the idea of them hooking up as a power couple.

But right now, Alyssa not only resented her intrusion. She also disliked the gleam of malice in Whitney's emerald green eyes as she took in their cozy, darkened table. "I was visiting a friend and decided to bring some dinner home. I had no idea the mayor kept such late office hours," she said with a tinkling laugh.

Alyssa cut in. "It's wonderful to see you, Whitney. Did you get the referral I sent you from the New York Mets?"

Her gaze narrowed. "That was you?"

"Of course. Micky is a friend of mine and said a few of his players would love to participate in some fundraising. I told him you were the best."

Her body relaxed slightly, like a predator suddenly distracted. "Thank you, Alyssa. I certainly do appreciate referrals."

"I'm afraid I had to drag poor Alyssa across town because I was craving carbs and refused to eat again in the office. Working and Italian food go together best, don't they?"

"Yes, they do. Watch out, Jonathan. I may have to steal her from you. She'd do amazing things for my foundation."

Jonathan laughed, then launched into a light chatter about mutual friends and the next big party. Finally, Whitney stepped back. "My food is ready, I must go. Always wonderful to see you. I'll call."

With long-legged grace, she walked out of the restaurant.

This time, the silence that came over the table wasn't comfortable. It held the edge of tension and the stink of reality.

Alyssa had been crazy to think they could try to have a secret relationship with no one catching them.

She cleared her throat and studied the cluttered table of half-eaten food and emptied wine glasses. The candle flickered, then grew bright again. "I think we should go now."

He muttered something under his breath. Frustration carved the lines of his face. "What are you thinking about?" he asked.

She looked him straight in the eye. "I think it's best if I go home."

His jaw clenched. He waited a few beats, then nodded. The bill was paid, and they were escorted to the car. The drive back to her apartment was different than the trip to the restaurant. They didn't speak but simmered with their own thoughts.

She got to her apartment and turned. "Thanks for dinner."

"I'll walk you up."

"No, I don't need—"

"I'll walk you up."

She shut her mouth and went through the awkward motions of climbing the stairs, getting her key, and heading to her door.

"I'd like to talk to you for a minute. Will you let me?"

Annoyance brushed her nerves. "Of course, you act like I'd be scared to let you into my house."

"I just want you to be comfortable around me. Always."

"Then stop acting like you're trying to convince me you're not a secret criminal about to pounce."

"Point taken."

They stepped through the door. She wondered what he thought of her place. He'd never been here. She tried to view it through his eyes and wondered if he liked it. The apartment was her personal treasure, with giant windows that let light pour in, and shiny oak floors that hinted at its age. Wood beams crisscrossed the ceiling, adding extra charm. The kitchen was cramped, the pipes clanked when the heat came on, and the closet space was limited, but she loved the airiness and pleasant charm. She especially liked that it had been bought by her own hand after endless hard work and a stoic ambition to finally own something for herself.

"Nice place," he commented, walking deeper into the room. He glanced at the multi-stone fireplace—still not working, but she was hopeful—and the cozy reading nook she'd put together, bookcases filling up one giant wall, and a lounger over a fuzzy white throw rug. "Have you read all these?" he asked, taking in her massive book collection.

"Yes. Those are my treasures. If I truly love a book, I buy it in hardcover or paperback. The rest are on my Kindle, where I can constantly pick and choose depending on my mood."

"And you like Scrabble?"

She wrinkled her nose. The brass trophy was a bit ostentatious, but she'd been proud of the tournament she'd won at the Strand bookstore, which had sponsored the event. "I like words. The way they feel on the tongue and sound to the ear. The way they're used to connect. The way they can be tweaked and changed into a lie or a truth, to either hurt or heal." She shrugged. "Words are constant."

"You can't say stuff like that, Alyssa, and expect me not to want to kiss you."

Her jaw almost dropped, but she caught it just in time. How could he stare at her with such hunger? As if at one touch, she'd be burned alive? How could she possibly inspire such passion from this man?

She did that terrible cliché thing she despised and licked her lips. "I was uncomfortable when Whitney saw us."

He let out a breath and jammed his fingers through his hair. "I know. Damnit, I didn't know how to play it. The idea of anyone trying to embarrass you killed me, so I spun it as a work dinner."

"Don't apologize, Jonathan. I wasn't expecting you to announce we were on a date. I just think we jumped in on impulse and hoped we'd be able to do this in secret for a while before deciding. But you're in the public eye. There is no privacy. And I don't want to see anything between us affect your election."

He tore at his tie as if he needed more breath. She itched to go over there and unknot it herself, slip it slowly off his collar, press her lips to his rough jaw, which held the slightest hint of shadow. She fisted her hands to stop herself.

"What if I don't care about the election?" he asked.

She never hesitated. "Well, I do."

They stared at one another. The energy crackled like a campfire devouring wood. He began to pace, and she walked to the desk, snatching up a hot pink stress ball and handing it over. He grabbed it, his fingers squeezing mercilessly as if they were about to solve a work problem rather than decide not to date. "What if I'm not ready to walk away from you yet? Want to hear something? I had the day from hell. I'm exhausted and stressed, and I won't be able to slow down until next November, but sitting across from you at that restaurant? I was happy—from the inside. I was happy for *me*, not pleased I did something for the city or the people, or for the job. You are my selfish comfort, Alyssa. When you walk into the office, my insides light up. So forgive me if I don't want to give you up after one date."

His words battered her, and suddenly, all those rational thoughts that always ruled her world crumbled under the raw need in his eyes when he looked at her. The silence was shattering.

"You can't say things like that and not expect me to kiss you," she said.

And suddenly, she was closing the distance and in his arms, rising up on tiptoes, and he was kissing her. And, dear God, she was drowning, held tight against his chest, his hands in her hair and his lips over hers. The blistering heat between them roared, exploded, and she opened her mouth under one perfect thrust of his tongue, starved for the taste of him.

His mouth was hot and damp and delectable. His tongue plunged deep, swirled, explored the cave of her mouth with a carnal hunger and a delicious precision that made her wet between her thighs. The scent of the ocean washed over her, and she whimpered as he nipped at her lower lip, his palms holding her face as he kissed her like she was the only woman he'd ever wanted.

Somehow, he walked her back until she hit the wall, and she slumped against it. Again and again, his mouth pressed, searched, played, while his hands dropped to explore, caressing down her hips to slide around her back and tug her even closer.

Gone. She was gone and never wanted to return. The smell and taste of him, the rough scrape of his jaw against her cheek, the burn of his palm under her buttocks as he lifted her so his thighs bracketed hers, and his erection notched perfectly against her throbbing center.

"I can't stop," he muttered, taking the kiss even deeper. "You taste so sweet."

"You taste like saltwater taffy," she murmured, sinking her fingers into the silky darkness of his hair, holding his head so he wouldn't stop. "My favorite treat at the boardwalk."

"Please don't ask me to walk away from this," he said, raining kisses down her cheek and neck, sinking his teeth carefully into the line of her shoulder. Her body shuddered with need, and she gave another moan, lifting her hips. "From us."

"This is only our first date," she panted, trying desperately to fight the cotton balls stuffed into her normally clear brain. "How can there be an us?"

"Because, for two years, we got to know each other. Bad and good. Weak and strong. It was like two years of foreplay," he growled, diving back in to tangle his tongue with hers.

"I don't know," she whispered, locking her arms around his neck. She surrendered then, not wanting to fight the pull of this man, the blazing heat of their attraction. "I can't think, Jonathan."

In that moment, she knew she was going to be dragged into her bedroom and finally have mind-blowing sex with the man of her fantasies. She had nothing left inside to shore up her defenses. The whole evening spun away, and when he tipped her chin up, she stared deep into his eyes, held there by a burning intensity that drove her breath away.

Then he was stepping back, turning away as he gulped a deep breath. She blinked, not understanding, while he re-knotted his tie and righted himself. "Alyssa, you mean more to me than a quick night. I won't do that unless you want to commit to trying to be with me."

"Like as your girlfriend?"

He winced at her high-pitched tone. "Yeah, as my girlfriend. I want a chance to show you how good we can be outside of the office. But I need you willing to try. And if I take you to bed tonight, you'll shut down on me."

Stunned, she realized he was right. She didn't do well with impulsive acts that she'd regret in the morning. The fact that he'd known and been able to stop them both told her she was more deeply involved than she'd ever thought.

He was a man she could so easily love if she let herself fall.

"I don't know."

"I do. So I'm going to head home, take a cold shower, and see you in the morning. And we'll take this step by step, slowly. But after that kiss, don't lie to me and say it's not worth it." He reached out and ran a finger down her cheek, smiling. "Good night, Alyssa."

He walked out and left her sexually frustrated, scared out of her mind, and something much, much worse.

Hopeful.

Chapter Six

She couldn't stop thinking about the kiss.

Alyssa stood to the side, positioned close to Jonathan's bodyguards and advising team while the press conference came to a close. He'd dazzled them all again with his confidence, strength, and passionate belief in issues that would only help the state. Education. The homeless. Restrictions on vaping. He wasn't a fan of legal marijuana, but the current governor was, so that was an issue he might need to compromise on. His movie-star looks only helped, giving him higher approval with both men and women. She knew appearance was a poor condition for being a good leader, but he'd been blessed and used it to his advantage.

She now knew, up close and personal, how those looks could affect a woman. His strength and piercing gaze, his firm mouth sliding so expertly over hers, heating up every inch of her body. Yet he wasn't a player, and not interested in bedding a long line of women—which would be easy with his position. No, he was moral from his political view to his soul, and that only made it harder to fight him.

"Who will you be taking to the Friends of Firefighters Gala, Mr. Mayor?" a reporter asked. "Are you still recovering from breaking up with Savannah Winters?"

Alyssa winced. Savannah was the latest television star who'd been seen a few times with Jonathan at social functions, but she'd moved on to begin dating a famous movie star. The press spun it as a cruel dumping and painted Jonathan as heartbroken for a full week of gossip. Alyssa knew it'd been nothing—they'd been friends—but having his love life pulled apart and analyzed was difficult to watch.

Hmm, the reporter was Diana Delaney. She'd been assigned to cover the mayor's office by a rag of a paper, but so far, she'd written quite fairly about Jonathan compared to what she penned about some other public officials. The lack of privacy was criminal and ridiculous, but Alyssa knew it was the price paid for political office. Fighting it didn't help, and accepting it with grace and firm boundaries was the only way to move forward.

"Does the city of New York really care about my lack of a dating life?" he teased, those blue eyes sparkling. He was adept at playing to the crowd, and a titter of laughter rang out. "Savannah is happy, and I wish her all the best. We're still good friends."

"Just curious. It's been how long since you've been married? Five years?"

His face suddenly tightened. A wary silence fell over the crowd as cameras flashed. "Yes," he finally said in a clipped voice. "But there's no time limit on the grief of losing a spouse, is there?"

Alyssa drew in a sharp breath. His late wife was always a vulnerable spot, but instead of jealousy, only tenderness rose within. He loved deeply, and he didn't choose often. If he loved her, it'd be with everything he had. Forever.

Her knees shook at the image of being able to claim him as hers. He deserved a woman who was strong and brave and could stand before a firestorm with her chin held high. Was she capable of being that type of partner? Or was it just a hopeless fantasy? Could she stand being in the public scrutiny day in and day out, even for him? Would she lose her identity to the power of his?

Her entire life revolved around being pushed into the spotlight against her will. And she couldn't live with herself if she affected his run for governor. The doubts had kept her from moving forward with him since the night of the kiss. He didn't push, but she sometimes saw the question burning in his gaze when he looked at her. When the day ended, and they were going their separate ways, he'd stop at her desk and stare at her in silence, waiting.

So far, she hadn't been able to answer. Not yet. She needed more time to figure things out.

The reporter's voice rose in the air amidst the crowd. "I apologize, Mr. Mayor."

Startled by the apology, she watched Jonathan visibly soften. "Accepted. Let's just say I won't be on the *Bachelor* anytime soon, okay? Now, let me get back to work. Thank you."

Alyssa fell into place within the procession as they left the press room.

The hours flew by in a frenzy of tasks and meetings until she was finally stumbling toward home. She couldn't wait to open the new political memoir that'd just hit the stands, sip a glass of wine, and cuddle under her favorite blanket. Every muscle in her body hurt from being on her feet nonstop, but the day had been productive, and a buzzing satisfaction zinged through her, giving her a natural high.

She'd just reached her place when she noticed the familiar black car waiting at the curb.

Jonathan stepped out, his dark wool coat only emphasizing his tall, lean body. He closed the distance between them, his aura practically pulsing with dynamic sexual energy. "What are you doing here? Is something wrong?" she asked with a frown, glancing at her phone to see if she'd somehow missed a text.

"I want you to go to the fireman's gala with me," he stated, stopping a few inches away.

She blinked. "You're asking me out on a date? In public? Officially?"

His jaw clenched. "Yes."

She shook her head, hard. "No, Jonathan, we're not ready for something like that. I told you, I need time."

He nodded, and she was surprised he'd accepted her refusal so easily. "I understand. I just want to say I'm not afraid of showing the world I'm interested in you. But if you won't go with me as my date, will you go as my assistant? My plus one? I can't show up alone to this one, and with you by my side, no one will question it."

She tilted her head and analyzed the pros and cons. She'd accompanied him to social events before, and no one had ever questioned them on a personal level. Maybe this would be a good way to gauge the public's reception if they officially began dating? Or perhaps it was just an excuse to be by his side rather than watch him take some other woman. Either way, it was safe enough for her to take a chance.

"Okay," she said. "I'll go with you."

He smiled. "Thanks, Alyssa. I'll pick you up at seven on Friday night?"

"Sure."

He leaned in. His breath brushed against her ear, causing her to shiver. "I haven't stopped thinking about that kiss or you. I just don't want you to forget that."

Then he pulled back. Got in his car. And drove away.

She stayed out on the curb, staring at the empty place where he'd been and knew she couldn't wait until Friday.

* * * *

"You look nice, Dad. Are you going with a date?"

He glanced over at his daughter. "You think I should wear the red tie instead for contrast? I don't look like Johnny Cash dressed all in black, do I?"

Chloe laughed. "No, it's a very cool look. I saw it on the Grammys."

"I better change."

He cherished her giggle and the easy way she was with him. God knew it had taken years for them to begin coming back together after losing Catherine, then dealing with the election. It was a gift to be able to talk on an equal footing. His baby was now a grown woman on her own career path and carving out a big, beautiful life. The pride when he looked into her blue eyes that matched his surged so deep, it became almost painful. "What are you doing tonight?" he asked, slipping on his dress shoes.

"Meeting a few friends in Chelsea for dinner and drinks. I just wanted to stop by and make sure we're still good for Thanksgiving."

He looked up and caught the faintest gleam of worry in her expression. Holidays were sometimes hard as mayor, and he'd missed a few with her for various reasons. This time, he'd pinky promised that unless it were a total crisis, he'd spend three entire days with her on holiday at the Robin's Nest B&B—the upstate inn with a horse rescue farm that Chloe had logged her community service hours at. The Bishops had become family to them, and Chloe visited regularly. She even had her own horse, Chloe's Pride, and Jonathan loved seeing her open and free and happy when she was there. It had even inspired her passion for animal welfare laws. It was the first time he'd be going there for the holiday, and he knew she was wary that he'd cancel.

"I promised, and I'm not going to break it," he said firmly, giving her a smile. "I'm looking forward to spending time together."

She let out a breath. "Good, because I have plans, and I know everyone wants to see you. But you can't spend all weekend plotting election publicity with Mia, okay?"

He laughed. As his head of PR, Mia had gone to the farm to watch over Chloe and ended up falling in love with Ethan Bishop and moving upstate permanently. But she was the best at her job, and they both had a tendency to work endless hours when they got together. "I promise. Ophelia's cooking, right?"

"Of course, no one else would be up to the task. I told her we'd bring all the wine, and I want to pick up one of those dried floral arrangements for the table." She chattered on about Thanksgiving, and horseback riding, and the local craft festival she wanted to attend, and for a little while Jonathan just relaxed and enjoyed his daughter's happiness. God, he wished Catherine could see her now.

Chloe stopped suddenly. "You thinking about Mom?" she asked softly.

He jerked slightly. He always forgot how perceptive to his mood she was. "Yeah. She would have been so damn proud of you, Chloe. You know that, right?"

She stepped into his arms and gave him a tight hug. "I know. You, too, Dad. This was her dream also, and governor is a pretty big deal. Just don't let it consume you."

He hugged her back. "I won't."

She stepped away and gave him a teasing look. "You didn't tell me who your date was. I think you're nervous."

He forced a laugh and finished buttoning his suit so he didn't have to look her in the face. "No date," he said lightly. "But Alyssa is going to accompany me."

"Dad!" Her tone brooked warning. "You didn't make her work on a Friday night, did you?"

"No! She wanted to. I mean, she accepted my invitation when I asked. She didn't mind at all."

Chloe rolled her eyes. "You two are attached at the hip, and I think you take advantage. Alyssa is so good at her job, you forget she should have a life of her own."

"Trust me, I wouldn't force her to do anything. I respect the heck out of her. This is a big social event, and I'm sure she'll have fun."

"Sure. What woman doesn't have fun following the mayor around and making sure everything goes smoothly? Why didn't you let her bring her own date?"

The thought made him want to growl, but he settled for a frown. "She's not seeing anyone. Why are you suddenly so concerned with Alyssa? Has she said something to you? Is she unhappy?"

"No, I just know she's a bit like Mia, and work can consume her. Ethan was able to balance Mia out and show her other things in life. I think Alyssa needs that, too. She's lonely."

He stared at his daughter. "You think she's lonely?"

She nodded. "Yeah, she doesn't see her parents, and she has no other family. I don't think she goes out much, either. What is she doing for Thanksgiving?"

The question knocked him off balance. The idea of Alyssa spending the holiday alone haunted him. "I don't know."

"I think we should invite her to the farm. There's plenty of room, and I think she would have a great time. What do you think?"

The idea hit him full-force. Having Alyssa with him in such a setting might be exactly what they both needed. Time away from the spotlight to really spend time with each other. He already knew she adored Chloe, and they talked consistently on their own. Having the two women who were most important to him together for a family weekend seemed like the biggest gift of all.

"I'll invite her," he said, trying to hide his excitement.

"Good, now I feel better. Have fun tonight."

"You, too, honey. Is there someone new in your life I need to know about yet?" he asked teasingly.

Her blue eyes filled with a flare of pain he knew all too well—one that spoke of heartbreak he wished he could save her from. "Not ready yet," she said, her forced smile not fooling him at all. "I want to be on my own for a while."

He squeezed her hand in reassurance. "It's hard to get over a first love," he said seriously. "I think it's great you're taking time for yourself and not rushing into anything because you're sad. Owen never deserved you anyway."

A choked laugh escaped her throat. "Dad, no boy will ever deserve me if it's up to you."

"Damn right."

She shrugged. "I can't be mad he chose his career over me. Long-distance relationships never work out anyway. He did me a favor by saving me another few years of dating just to be dumped."

"I can do a lot of things to him, Chloe," he said. "Bad things. My reach as mayor is more than you know."

That got a real smile out of her. "Aww, thanks, Dad. I'll keep it in mind. For now, though, cocktails and girlfriends sound just about perfect."

She gave him a wink and headed out.

He checked his watch, not wanting to be late to pick Alyssa up. By the time he got to her door, he realized he was sweating more than usual. Like a nervous teen. Humiliating. He ran a city, and yet this slip of a woman affected him like no other. What amazed him was the way he was still able to separate his personal feelings in the office. She helped him run City Hall with a tight grip and ruthless organization that kept his brain in the game, but the moment the clock struck five, his dick seemed to wake up like Cinderella's magic spell.

Because then, it was his time.

He climbed the steps, but she was already stepping out, marching determinedly toward him like they were about to embark on a meeting rather than a ball. Her practical black coat gapped open just enough for him to spot the classic black cocktail dress she wore, but it was what was left off that made him speechless.

The hem of her dress stopped a bit higher than usual, leaving a good solid inch above the knee, flashing long, bare legs that ate up the distance with a no-nonsense pace. She stopped in front of him and tilted her head back. "Hi. Why are you looking at me like that?"

Damn, she was beautiful. Those large, almond-shaped eyes behind her glasses shimmered with an emotion he craved to tap. Her scent danced around him, cool and clean and crisp. Her dirty-blond hair was swept up on top of her head, but this time, she'd let some loose curls dangle around her temples, softening her face. The hints were subtle, but he'd made it his job to begin learning everything about Alyssa Block he possibly could, and every sign pointed to the fact that she'd dressed for him tonight.

As a woman. Not an employee.

"You look amazing," he said, lifting her hand and pressing a kiss to her palm. Her fingers shook in his, and he hid a smile, pleased by her reaction.

An elegant snort escaped her plump, glossy lips. "I look the same exact way I always do."

"I agree. Beautiful."

He ignored her adorable, doubting frown and escorted her into the car. "Tell me how your day was," he said.

She crossed her legs, then tugged her coat down to make sure she was covered up. He found the gesture charming. "I went to an off-Broadway play currently in previews."

"By yourself?"

She tossed him a look. "Yes, by myself. Is there something wrong with that? I happen to like my own company."

He grinned. "Not at all, I love that you take yourself where you want to go. Too many of us are dependent on others or our phones for distraction. Was the play good?"

"Yes, it was a dark comedy but more clever than I expected." She launched into the analysis of the plot and characterization. He felt as if he'd seen the play himself by the time she was done.

"Do you get your love of theater from your parents?"

"Probably. Growing up in the lifestyle, you gain some appreciation for it. It never made sense why they didn't like books when all plays are based on scripts, but they seemed to look at performance differently."

"They never read to you when you were little?"

"No. They preferred movies and performances over words, citing books were too stringent and allowed for no creative mental freedom. It drove them crazy that I was such a bookworm."

His heart squeezed in sympathy. Her parents didn't seem abusive, just selfish about what they wanted rather than their only child. Imagining her growing up as a lonely misfit made him want to fold her in his arms and comfort her. "I'm sorry. One of my favorite memories when I was a child was my mother reading *Green Eggs and Ham*."

She snapped to attention. "Did you know Dr. Seuss wrote that exclusively to win a bet? He was told he couldn't write a story with only fifty different words, so Seuss took the bet. Fifty dollars was on the line."

He had to hold himself back from caressing her cheek or touching her in some way. She was charming when she recited her knowledge. "He won a lot more than fifty bucks after he wrote that, huh?"

"Yes. Anyway, unlike my parents, I find most stories fascinating because perspectives and outlooks differ depending on who's watching."

"You always term your mind as linear, but I think you have a wealth of creativity. Did you ever think about writing reviews or even a book?"

She shook her head. "I'm afraid I'd go too deep in my head and miss out on the pleasure of being a participant. I don't want to risk it."

"Makes sense. Sometimes doing the things we love professionally kills the joy."

"Exactly. What did you do today?"

"Boring errands mostly. Chloe stopped by."

He adored the way her face lit up. "How is she?"

"Good, she was heading out with friends tonight. Wanted to check on her old man."

"Is she still struggling with her breakup with Owen?"

His heart warmed at her concern for his daughter. "I think so, but she didn't want to admit it. If I see that boy around one day, I'll tear him apart."

She grinned, and his insides lit up. "You raised a daughter who doesn't need her father to fight her battles. She'd probably do more damage to Owen than you ever could."

"I think you're right. Speaking of Chloe, we talked about Thanksgiving. What are your plans?"

A tiny frown creased her brow. "Well, I'm planning to relax, eat a turkey by myself, and catch up on my reading. Why? Do you need me to volunteer at one of the shelters? I can definitely do that, Jonathan, especially since you won't be here."

He waved his hand in the air. "No, we have that covered. I have a team in place to hit a few of the soup kitchens in the area, and they know I'll be away for the weekend. Chloe and I want you to join us at the Bishop farm this year."

Shock flickered over her face. "I-I can't do that. It's a family dinner. But thank you for the invite."

"Alyssa, we want you there. Chloe asked for you specifically, and it would be a great favor if you came. She misses her mother the most around the holidays, and you and she have become close. You make her happy. And the Bishop farm is a free-for-all. I know you'd love it there. Your schedule has been just as insane as mine, and I think we both need a break."

She blinked rapidly, and he watched her process the idea. "I don't know."

"It's a getaway—completely private. Ethan has bodyguards at the place, and with my team on-site, we'll be out of the public eye. You can ride horses, hike, be in the great outdoors without the smog and smoke and pavement." He smiled. "And you'll get to hang out with Chloe and Mia. Meet Mia's sisters—Ophelia and Harper. See the famous racehorse, Phoenix."

"You're really selling this place, aren't you?"

He grinned. "Guess I am. Will you think about it? I think Chloe needs some extra female support after the breakup with Owen. It would mean everything to her if you'd go."

A sigh escaped her lips. "It does sound beautiful, and I'd do anything for Chloe. I'll think about it."

"Good."

They smiled at each other, then pulled up to the Prince George Hotel. The Friends of Firefighters Fall Gala was a well-publicized event and supported the local Breaking Ground nonprofit, which helped give affordable housing to New Yorkers. Since homelessness was a big issue for him, he supported the organization as much as possible, and combined with honoring the city's brave firefighters, it was a win/win.

They made their way inside. He loved the Neo-Renaissance features of the renovated hotel. It reminded him of age-old glamour. The ballroom was exquisite. The fat columns of scrolled gold, gleaming wooden floors, and dazzling painted tray ceiling made one feel as if they'd stepped back into aristocratic history. He stopped to talk to the fire chief, and the men he'd come to know and respect, those who woke up every morning with the heavy images of 9/11 in their brains and hearts, yet still showed up to give their lives to save another's. Jonathan's relationship with the fire stations and crew was important to him, and he'd fought many times to get them more funding and support, even when he was up against the budget and endless other causes.

He worked the room with Alyssa by his side. He admired the way she handled the crowds, a subtle, stable presence, ready to infuse humor or bring a fresh take to an issue. She was more comfortable in the background, and there was always respect in his role as mayor, but when their gazes met, he knew they were on equal ground. She was secure in herself and strong in her identity, and that was important. God knew he'd been known to intimidate and dominate women with his personality. He never wanted to worry that his partner would be in his shadow.

Alyssa was perfect for him in all ways.

He only hoped she felt the same way about him.

They eased away from the latest crowd and shared a glance. It was tradition for them to spend the first half-hour getting settled with the crowds, then bolt for a cocktail and a small bite to sustain themselves for the next few hours. "Chardonnay?" he asked.

"Yes, and if you see those little—"

"Crab cakes? I'll grab some and get cheese and crackers."

"Perfect, I'll hit up the library association members standing by that column and remind them of your support."

"I'll tackle Ted, who's at the bar with his cronies. Meet you in the back-right corner for the exchange in fifteen."

She wrinkled her nose. "Get real. Thirty minutes minimum. Ted's a talker."

"And I'm a professional." He quirked a brow. "Care to bet? I'll be there in fifteen, and if I'm not, you get to ask for a favor."

"You didn't say you'd grant it. Only that I get to ask."

Damn, he was nuts about her. "You should have been a lawyer. Okay, I'll grant any favor you wish, if it's possible. If I win, you reciprocate and grant me a boon."

Interest sparked in her brown eyes. She pushed her glasses back up her nose. "Hmm, that's too good to resist. Done."

"If you get there and I'm talking with Sam Walterson, please—"

"I'll cite an emergency and get you out of there. I'm a professional, too, Mr. Mayor." This time, the tone in her voice when she called him by his official title was in fun and took on an intimacy he wanted more of. He couldn't resist teasing her back a tiny bit.

"Thanks. And don't forget, Alyssa." He leaned over and growled near her ear. "If I'm on time, be ready for what I'm going to ask for."

Then, with a grin, he headed to the bar.

The clock was ticking.

* * * *

He was on time.

She came up behind him, watching him chat casually with two ladies who seemed to gush over every word he uttered. He sipped a scotch with ice, and a plate of appetizers sat on the high table to his left.

He turned to look at her, and that tingle between her thighs bolted to a lightning strike. Thank God her bra was industrial strength because her nipples were hard knots under the padding. How did a man exude such graceful strength and sensual energy, just by zeroing in with those piercing blue eyes? His entire body vibrated with a leashed power she craved to let loose. The kiss was proof that he'd dominate her in the bedroom—body and soul. She also knew if they kissed again, she'd never be able to stop.

"Alyssa." He caressed her name, his smile warm as if only for her.

"Thank goodness. I apologize, ladies, but I need a few minutes alone with my able assistant."

The pair smiled at her and happily drifted off. He handed her the chardonnay, his gaze holding hers. "I won."

She waited, taking a sip as the chattering crowd seemed to drop away for a few precious moments. "How?"

His lower lip tugged. "Does it matter? Will you grant my favor?"

"Depends on what it is," she retorted, enjoying their banter. She nibbled on her crab cake. "I won't do anything illegal."

He looked delighted by her answer. "Even if I promised you clemency?"

"You can't, you don't have that type of power."

"I will when I'm governor."

"Then if it's an illegal activity, you can wait to collect until after you win the election."

He laughed out loud. Lord, he was sexy when he did that. The creases around his eyes deepened, and his white teeth flashed, and she wished she could make him laugh all day long, just for her pleasure. Instead, she ate her cheese and crackers, knowing their time alone was about to end. The music was in full swing, an array of gentle pop and slow songs, and the dance floor was full of couples taking advantage of the gorgeous, romantic atmosphere before the official speeches and awards were given out.

His voice softened, and he lowered his head toward her. "I think you already know what I want to ask, Alyssa."

She stilled, took another sip of her wine, then slammed him back with her gaze. "I'm not ready to answer yet."

He gave a tight nod. She watched him struggle for his next words, seeming to sift through some to pick the perfect ones for their rapidly decreasing time limit. "It's your favorite song."

She blinked. "What?"

His head jerked toward the dance floor. "The Chainsmokers. That's the concert you went to recently, right?"

He remembered. She'd gone with a few women from work who'd scored tickets, but in the darkened auditorium, with the creative and emotional lyrics ringing in her ears, she'd been alone with her heart and soul open, the music taking her somewhere else. "Yes."

"What's this called?"

The music took her back to the time they'd played this. And how she'd thought of him. "*Something Just Like This*. But they collaborated on this song with Coldplay."

"One of my favorite bands. They seem to make an incredible team." He slowly held out his hand. "Dance with me."

She tried to speak, but no words came out. Her heart pounded ridiculously fast. "No, Jonathan, we can't. People may talk."

A gentle smile curved his mouth. "Just one dance, Alyssa. And then we'll get back to safety and dazzle the crowds and the press and pretend we're not dying to touch each other. We'll lie and say this is just about work and not emotions I haven't felt in over five years. I want to hold you for a little while and pretend you're mine in front of all these people. Can you do that? As my favor?"

A shudder wracked her. Alyssa knew she had to say no. It was dangerous to put herself on a public dance floor, vulnerable to the crowd's stare. Everyone would see how she really felt about the mayor, and it would all blow up. But, unbelievably, her heart won the battle.

She took his hand and followed him to a small empty space in the center of the floor.

His arm slipped around her waist, and one hand enclosed hers. They held a respectable distance between their bodies as he began to move, but his blue eyes blistered with pure heat. Her fingers curled into his shoulder, the meaty muscle under his sleek suit jacket clenching under her grip. Her bare legs brushed against his pants. The dress that had seemed like decent armor before melted like newspaper under flame, her body warming and softening with every step they took around the floor. Somehow, she had enough brain matter left to nod at other dancers, making it look as if the dance were a nice gesture from the mayor instead of the sexual inferno rising between them.

The Chainsmokers sang about not needing a superhero to love, and Jonathan kept an easy smile on his face like the dance meant nothing but a social nicety, but she knew it was so much more when he looked at her. The fierce plea was there. If she said yes, he'd pull her close, bury his face in her hair, and let the world do as it may. They'd be plastered on page six, she'd be hounded by the press, and he'd have endless closed-door meetings with the governor and Mia's PR team about how badly he'd handled coming out with his assistant.

For one moment, Alyssa wished she were a different type of woman. One who took risks and was adventurous at heart. But she wasn't. She was a rule follower, saw too much of the big picture and the statistics of disaster, and refused to take the leap.

For one moment, she became that woman. She leaned in close, studying Jonathan's perfect chiseled jaw, strong brow, and fierce eyes. She breathed him in, relished the blistering body heat pulsing through his shirt, practically heard the rapid beat of his heart. His carved lips were pure temptation, and now she knew how good they felt whispering over hers, his tongue plunging into her mouth, his masculine taste better than the sweet taffy she'd obsessed over as a child.

He whispered her name.

She stepped back.

The music stopped.

There was no time for anything else. People swept in immediately, separating them, chattering about nonsense and politics and fundraising and a bunch of other subjects that meant nothing to her. At least, not now.

She drifted away, needing space, and headed toward the ladies' room. It took her a while to get there since she made sure to chat like nothing monumental had occurred while dancing with her boss, and finally reached the cool, darker space of a temporary sanctuary.

Locking herself in a stall, she calmed down and pulled herself together. Smoothed her dress and tugged down her skirt. When she walked back to the sinks, she looked less ruffled and rummaged in her purse to reapply her gloss.

Heels tapped on the floor. Her gaze met Whitney's in the mirror, the woman's cold green eyes hinting at the unpleasantness about to come. Alyssa held back a groan. Now? She had to deal with this woman when she was at her most vulnerable, trying to pretend she wasn't half in love with the mayor, the most eligible bachelor of New York?

Fantabulous.

Using a word that wasn't really a word soothed her. She forced herself to pretend they were about to have a normal conversation. "Hello, Whitney. So nice to see you."

"You, too, Alyssa. Did you enjoy the dance?"

She tried not to stiffen. Yep, this was going to be bad. Whitney had been after Jonathan for a while, and his disinterest only made her more rabid to change his mind. Her silver dress sparkled and clung to her curvy body, finished off with a pair of metallic stilettos that probably cost more than Alyssa's entire wardrobe. Hip cocked out, lips pursed like she'd scented something bad, the woman's gaze raked over Alyssa in scorching dismissal.

Good thing it didn't bother her. She already knew what Whitney saw since she looked at her reflection in the mirror every morning. Honestly, she didn't care. She wouldn't want to look like Whitney or be her anyway. The only time she'd stumbled was at the restaurant when the thought of Jonathan preferring someone like her crumbled her heart into tiny pieces.

"The dance? With Jonathan. Yes, he's a good dancer," she said blandly.

A sparkly laugh escaped the woman's cherry-red lips. "Oh, you're good. I think I may have underestimated you, after all. But though Jonathan may enjoy a roll on the desk, please don't be mistaken about his true intentions. He's running for governor. A scandal with his secretary would ruin him."

She arched a brow. "Assistant. And I agree. Therefore, I'm not sure what you're trying to say."

Surprise skittered across Whitney's features. Then her green eyes hardened. "You know exactly what I'm saying. Jonathan and I have been dating secretly for a while. I'm not about to stand around while you try to destroy a burgeoning career and relationship that actually means something." Whitney washed her hands, dried them, and checked her hair in the mirror. "Now, let's put this unpleasantness behind us, shall we? I'd be happy to offer you another employment opportunity running the Stoker Foundation. They're looking for a new director, and they always listen to my recommendations."

Shock barreled through her. Not that Whitney wasn't above bribery to keep Jonathan to herself, but that she felt that threatened by Alyssa. Had she seen something in Jonathan's eyes that tipped her off?

"That's a top-rate position," she said. "I'm impressed."

"Good. Women need to stick together, Alyssa, not tear each other down. I'll arrange a call for an interview on Monday." She flashed a charming, shark-like smile and nodded as if they'd just completed a business meeting. "I knew you were smart. You'll do well with the company, and deserve a higher salary than a public servant."

A group of women came in, laughing, and Whitney disappeared like a silent serpent.

Alyssa smiled pleasantly at the women and headed back to the ballroom, her thoughts spinning. Whitney deemed her dangerous enough to offer her an extremely good position to leave City Hall. Had she missed something deeper between Whitney and Jonathan? He had stated a few times that he wasn't interested, but was Whitney desperate enough to lie?

Either way, she couldn't keep playing this dangerous game. She needed to commit to exploring a relationship with Jonathan, or close and lock the door forever. It wasn't fair to lead him on, especially if he had the opportunity to meet a woman who'd fit into his life and help his run for governor.

Her throat tightened with emotion, and a hard knot settled in her chest. She didn't want to lose him, but she didn't want to risk him losing the governor seat either. Sure, there were worse scandals that broke with officials still being elected. Lord knew Trump had made affairs and mistakes like a television drama with high ratings, and Jonathan was widowed—not married. He was free to date whomever he chose.

It was her current work role in the #metoo movement that concerned her. He'd open himself up for questions about being inappropriate in the office, and she'd be endlessly grilled about the personal and professional lines they'd agreed on. It might cause doubt, and enough bad press for the opposing candidate to step right through the door, especially since he was married with a solid family behind him.

Alyssa made sure to keep her distance for the rest of the evening. Eventually, she'd have to deal with Whitney because there was no way she was taking a job that woman offered—no matter how good it was. But if she stayed, she needed to be clear it was strictly business between Jonathan and her from now on. Or take the plunge and see how the pieces fell.

The hours dragged by, and she caught Jonathan's puzzled looks when he tried to talk to her, and she deliberately disappeared or stepped right into a busy crowd to jump into a new conversation. By the end of the night, it was obvious that she was avoiding him, and even more clear that he was pissed.

When they got back into the car, they both kept their silence. No need for Tim to bear witness to the feud brewing between them. With each mile closer to her apartment, Alyssa felt her stomach lurch with nausea, but she'd made her decision.

Tonight, she had to tell him.

Then she had to live with it.

Chapter Seven

He was losing her.

The silence in the car screamed with tension, and poor Tim had turned on the radio to keep from hearing it. Something had changed after their dance. The connection between them had buzzed so strongly, his confidence had risen to almost inhuman levels at the certainty that she was ready to take a leap with him. The emotions twisted his insides and throbbed beneath the surface, desperate to live in the light. He believed they both deserved a shot at happiness. But when she'd returned later, there had been a distance, and a tension carved out in her feminine features that he couldn't break through. The way she'd avoided him the rest of the night had sent him into a panic.

Had someone confronted her?

Or had the raw truth been too much for her to take?

He knew he wasn't an easy man to be with, let alone love. Too many strings bound him to a career in public service that many women weren't fit for. But Alyssa had evolved from a skilled assistant to his entire support system. How could he let her walk away?

By the time they pulled up to her apartment, they were both ready to jump out of the car and their skin. When she turned to face him, sadness bruised her eyes behind those signature lenses. "Jonathan? Can I speak with you a moment inside?"

The formality almost broke him. Unable to speak, he followed her in.

She dragged in a breath. "I have something important to say."

"Alyssa?" His voice broke around her name.

She closed her eyes halfway as if afraid to hear anymore. "Yes?"

"Are you giving up before we even started?"

His question demanded things from her he prayed she'd embrace.

But his heart already knew the answer as she tipped her chin up and looked him straight in the eye while she said the one word he wasn't ready for.

"Yes."

He let out a blistered curse, reached out before realizing he didn't have the right to touch her, then stumbled back. "Did something happen tonight? I noticed a change after our dance."

"Whitney spoke with me in the restroom."

Another curse escaped. Damn Whitney. She'd been hot on his trail for a while now, ambition twisted with lust in her eyes for a political spouse spot, and she hadn't been subtle. But neither had he. He'd made his intentions clear. He wasn't interested in pursuing her. "Nothing is going on between Whitney and me. I told her straight out a long time ago."

"I know. She tried to insinuate you'd been seeing each other, but I sensed it was a bluff. She bribed me with another high-level job if I left your office."

He ground his teeth as anger pounded through him. "How dare she? I swear to God, Alyssa, I'm going to have a talk with her. That's unacceptable."

She waved her hand wearily in the air. "It doesn't matter. Let it go, I'm not taking the bribe. But she did make her intentions known about exposing us. I guess she saw the way I looked at you during the dance."

"She probably saw the way I looked at you."

Alyssa flinched. He ached to close the distance between them and apply his usual determination to win her over. Kiss her, strip her, fuck her. Keep her tied to his bed for so many hours, she'd finally surrender and admit that she wanted him and damn the consequences. But Alyssa was stronger than most, and he knew she needed to be the one to decide.

"I know you want to take a chance," she said softly. "But I'm not risking it. I'll continue working for you, but it has to be business from here on out. We both have too much to lose."

He pinned her with his stare. The air squeezed with sexual tension and unspoken emotion. "Or maybe we both win."

A strangled laugh escaped her throat. "I knew you wouldn't give up easily."

"We're not doing anything wrong, Alyssa. I'm willing to put it out there for the world, and I don't give a crap what anyone thinks. Let them judge or pick us apart or write junk in a paper. As long as I have you, I can fight them all. Don't let Whitney scare you away from something this good."

"I'm not. I'm looking at the bigger picture. Am I just supposed to step from the role of valued assistant to bed partner? Do you know how bad that will look?"

Irritation bristled. "It's not like that, and you know it. You'd be my lover. My girlfriend. My cherished partner. Take your pick."

"The press would pigeonhole me. Rip away my skills and talents and everything I've accomplished by insinuating I slept my way to the top. Do you think, even in this day and age, it's safe for a woman to succeed? It's not, Jonathan. People are always looking to strip us from our pedestal, and the moment we win something, the world can't wait to rip it away like we'll never be worthy. It's different for you. It always has been."

God, he hated that she was right. Despised that he'd be deemed a conquering hero, and her the villainess, or a slut, or a social climber. Even worse? Someone who used sex to succeed. He'd tear the press and critics apart if they ever tried to spin such crap, which would end up feeding the entire media circus.

And she knew it.

The grim knowledge in her eyes ripped him apart. She was right. She saw things he couldn't because of his role. And if he kissed her, tried to bend her to his will and make her believe it would all be okay, she might lose a part of herself she'd never be able to heal.

He couldn't be the man to do that.

A terrible sense of grief filled him from the inside. Could he work so closely with her, day in and day out, knowing Alyssa Block would never be truly his? Could he step aside while she found a man who could be her partner in every way? Could he pretend he wasn't half in love with her and stick to business?

He had to. For her. There was no other choice.

He studied her beautiful face in the shadows, wishing things were different. For the first time, he wished he'd never been offered the opportunity to run for governor because maybe he could have had her instead.

Slowly, he nodded. "I understand. You know, I read something in this fact book and thought of you. It said the loneliest creature on Earth is a whale who's been calling out for a mate for over two decades. But he can't find one because his voice is so different to other whales that they never respond. It made me so damn sad."

"Jonathan—"

The sound of his name on her lips almost drove him to his knees. He stood at the door, his heart eroding like clumps of sand breaking apart in a fisted hand. "You're so smart. And beautiful. And funny. You're pretty much everything I never knew I wanted."

"I'm sorry."

He dragged in a ragged breath. "I know. I promise I won't make this harder on you. Your job is sacred, and I'll never ask again."

He waited for her to say something, anything, but she just stared at him and slowly nodded.

He turned away and left.

He didn't look back.

* * * *

Two weeks passed, and every day, Alyssa questioned her decision.

They fell back into a normal routine, but nothing would ever be the same between them. A barrier had been ripped away, and she'd caught a glimpse of what could have been hers. Every time she glanced at his chiseled profile or the weary sadness in his jeweled blue eyes, she was reminded. It was torturous, but he'd kept his promise. He didn't treat her any differently, didn't subtly try to punish her or distance himself. She was still at his side, managing every aspect of his day, expertly dealing with the burgeoning media requests along with a cycle of big-name contacts who wanted a piece of him and the election. She was still challenged and respected.

The only difference was her heart, which was no longer whole.

Alyssa tamped down a sigh and began packing up for the day. She was exhausted after back-to-back meetings and a crisis with accounting, so she'd pick up takeout and collapse.

Thanksgiving loomed, and she tried to push the thought of another lonely holiday away. The last holiday, she'd joined Jonathan in the soup kitchen, serving dinner for the homeless. It still ranked as her favorite. Watching him interact in worn jeans and a flannel shirt, joking as he served stuffed pots full of food classics, refusing to let cameras in to film because it would threaten the privacy of the same people he'd come to support. Alyssa wondered if that was when she realized she wished he was hers. Chloe had joined him one year to help serve, but she'd been asking her father to go to the Bishop farm, and he'd finally agreed. It'd be good for them to have some bonding time. Knowing she'd be missing him, she'd even reached out to her parents, desperate for a distraction, but they were on the road.

She refused to sulk. Usually, she loved a quiet holiday to do all the things she enjoyed. She had two full days off, which was unheard of, and needed to take advantage.

The phone rang, and she picked it up automatically. "City Hall, mayor's office."

"Alyssa! It's Chloe."

She smiled at her voice. "Hi. How's it going?"

"Pretty good. I've been working on this huge case that could really make a difference for animal rights, but there're so many layers of bullshit I can't get through."

"Welcome to the law. Your father could probably help, you know. He's pretty damn good at that."

Chloe laughed. "I know, but I want to try and figure this out on my own. Anyway, I'm calling to see if you're driving up with Dad. What time do you estimate arrival? I figured I'd go directly to you since you're always in charge of his schedule anyway."

Confusion flickered. "I'm sorry, drive up where? He's got nonstop appointments until six p.m. the day before Thanksgiving."

"I figured. Okay, why don't you leave early enough so we have the whole day together? Maybe we can ride before dinner."

"Umm, I don't understand, Chloe. Your father is heading to the farm for the holiday, right?"

"Yeah, but you're coming with him. I checked with him weeks ago, and he confirmed you were joining us."

A roaring sound buzzed in her ears. Was he insane? She opened her mouth to tell Chloe there was a misunderstanding, but the girl was excitedly chattering. "I can't wait to see you! I've got a great itinerary planned for us, and you'll get to meet Phoenix and my horse, and finally try one of Ophelia's famous blueberry scones!"

Alyssa's heart galloped like a racing thoroughbred, and sweat prickled her skin. Oh, no. How could Jonathan do this? She'd told him she'd think about it, but that was before they decided to keep things professional between them. How could she spend an entire weekend alone with him?

"Listen, Chloe, I forgot to tell you—"

"Do you know this is the first sit-down Thanksgiving dinner we've had since my mom passed? I avoided it for a while, happy that Dad and I were busy with soup kitchens or work or anything to keep me from thinking about missing her. But this year is different. I feel like being with you and Dad and the Bishops will be kind of…healing. Anyway, I already told Dad to just bring the wine, nothing else is needed because Ophelia goes nuts with the shopping. And I'm bringing the apple cider donuts. I can't wait to see you. Text me when you guys leave, okay? Make sure he doesn't work too late on Wednesday!"

Alyssa's throat closed up in a panic. "Well—"

"Oops, gotta go, my boss is coming. See you soon!"

The phone clicked.

Her trembling hands let the receiver drop. This was not happening. She was absolutely not going upstate with Jonathan Lake. Not for a million dollars. Not for all the tea in China. Not for world peace.

She grumbled under her breath and marched into his office.

He was bent over his desk, focused on the screen in front of him, his fingers ruthlessly clenching the stress ball in his palm as he muttered to himself. He looked up in surprise—she never walked in without knocking or announcing—and she slammed the door behind her.

"I just got a call from Chloe about what time we were leaving on Thanksgiving to drive to the farm."

His eyes closed. "Ah, shit."

"Yeah, *ah shit*!" She jabbed her finger in the air. "Did you tell her I was coming with you?"

"I think so. I don't remember. I think I said I'd asked and then forgot to tell her you changed your mind."

"I never said yes, Jonathan. I said I'd think about it! She was all excited and happy and now you're going to have to give some excuse why I'm not there."

He rubbed his hands over his face and leaned back in his chair. "Alyssa, I'm sorry, I screwed up. It's just been a bit…hard lately."

She stilled, daring a glance at him. His suit was slightly rumpled, and weariness etched his features. God, he needed a break. They'd both been working day and night, trying nonstop to keep things neutral between them, which was slowly breaking them apart, piece by piece. The anger drained away. He hadn't been trying to manipulate her. "What are we going to say?"

"Crap. She was looking so forward to seeing you. I can't use work as an excuse, or she'll never talk to me again."

The memory of Chloe's words about missing her mother ripped

through her. She'd never felt like a maternal figure before, but for some reason, the two of them had bonded easily. What if Chloe really needed her? "She mentioned how happy she was to have a traditional holiday again," she finally said. "How much it meant to her."

He nodded. "Yeah, we haven't been interested in sitting at a table for a long time. Too many memories. But this year, she seemed to need that bonding again. She's beginning to heal." His blue gaze snapped up, driving into her soul. "Alyssa, will you consider coming with us? For Chloe? There's plenty of room and space, and I promise not to get in your way. You can spend some time at the farm, and it will be a mini-vacation for you, too."

She hesitated. It was dangerous, but she wanted to be there for Chloe. After all, there were plenty of people to distract them, and she'd make sure she stayed away from Jonathan. She could take a break, help in the kitchen, spend some time getting to know the Bishop women, and maybe return stronger. Perhaps this could be a test, a way to convince herself they could co-exist without her heart being slowly torn apart.

"Do you think we can handle it?" she asked.

For one moment, raw hunger sizzled from his gaze, a naked need that made her knees sag and her blood thicken. Then it was gone, locked safely behind a tight smile and a determined nod. "Yeah. I won't touch you. I'll keep my distance. Okay?"

She hated the promise and fought the impulse to cross the room, sit in his lap, and take him in her arms. Beg him to kiss her and take back the words that should have soothed rather than tortured. But she was strong, and he was only doing what she'd asked. She'd given up her right to expect anything more.

"I'll go."

His shoulders relaxed. "Thank you. It will mean so much to Chloe."

"No. Thank you for inviting me. I'm the one who's lucky to have such an extraordinary young woman care about me."

The distance between them shattered. The air thickened. She made out his ragged breaths, practically heard the crazy beat of his heart as they stared at one another, the words hanging heavily in the silent room.

He ripped his gaze away and cleared his throat. "Very good. Make sure my schedule is clear so we can both leave on time."

"Of course, Mr. Mayor."

She walked out, refusing to be hurt by the rules she'd put in place.

Chapter Eight

When Alyssa arrived at the Robin's Nest B&B, she felt as if she'd entered a hidden sanctuary, destined to pamper travelers with warmth, good food, and charm.

When she arrived at the horse rescue farm attached to the B&B, she felt as if she'd entered a Disney movie.

The farm was located in the Hudson Valley region, which boasted mighty mountains, twisted country roads, and offered stunning views of the Hudson River. Gardiner was a small town full of shops, cafés, and farm stands, offering a variety of fresh fruits, vegetables, and baked goods. Apple picking was huge, along with specially crafted beer and wine trails to rival Napa. As she took her first walk to the barn area after settling in at the inn, the Shawangunk mountains rose before her at the edge of the valley, halfway hidden by low-riding clouds. The muted colors of earthy brown, rust, and forest green contrasted with the moody blue-gray sky. Even the air rushed in her lungs differently, clean and crisp and chilled. The scents of earth, oak, and apples rolled into one, reminding her of the first whiff of a perfect chardonnay.

It was paradise.

"Told you," Chloe squealed, taking in the look on her face. "It's beautiful, right?"

"Now I understand why you're drawn here," she said, her boots kicking up dried leaves and gravel. "You're a city girl reborn."

"Just don't quit your job and run one of those dude ranches,"

Jonathan cut in, tugging on his daughter's braid. "Or I'll have to kill Ethan for putting the idea in your head."

"It'd be a dudette ranch, Dad," she teased back. "And Ethan is more hardcore than you about my job. He said it's not just a calling. It's a necessity to protect the animals who can't fight for themselves."

"I'd say Ethan finally got one thing right."

Alyssa cocked her head, wondering if Jonathan was jealous of his daughter's affection for the man who'd introduced her to the horse rescue farm, but there was only a look of gentle laughter on his face.

Chloe practically skipped down the trail like Tigger. Alyssa loved seeing her so animated. "I want to introduce you to a few of the rescue animals here. Harper was able to expand the farm and the property after Phoenix almost won the Triple Crown, so now they house more animals for rehabilitation and adoption. Oh, that's Phoenix over in the field."

She pointed to a sleek, smaller type thoroughbred, black as night, with a zigzag of white on his forehead. The famous horse had come from fifty-to-one odds to win the Breeders' Cup Juvenile as a two-year-old, then had moved on to the Kentucky Derby and Belmont Stakes, capturing America's hearts forever. A goat stuck right to his side as they munched on hay together, seeming to soak in the final rays of sun on this early winter afternoon. "Is that Captain Hoof?"

"Yep, they're rarely apart."

Alyssa had heard about the half-blind goat who'd been rescued by Harper and her husband, Aidan, then slowly bloomed to health on the farm. The goat's journey had seemed fated to bond with Phoenix, who needed a calming companion on the road when he raced at the various tracks. She smiled as she looked out at the pair. They reminded her of an old married couple in their twilight years.

A whistle cut through the air. Alyssa turned to see a very tall, dark-haired woman making her way across the pasture. Phoenix and Captain Hoof looked up, then obediently began trotting after her as she led them toward the barn. "Chloe, can you lock up barns six and seven for me?" the woman asked. "Aidan's on his way home, and I still have to stop in and feed the dogs and Figaro."

"Of course. I was just giving my dad and Alyssa a brief tour before we head to the inn."

Harper smiled and reached out her hand. She wore no makeup, and her green eyes gleamed with a calm light of happiness that immediately put Alyssa at ease. "Nice to meet you. Chloe's been dying to have you up here for a while. Gonna do some horseback riding?"

"Going to try," Alyssa said, smiling back.

"We'll get you a gentle one. How are you, Mr. Mayor? Have you and Mia settled on a plan to take over the world?"

Jonathan laughed. "I'll settle for the state. Mia can have the rest."

Phoenix nipped at Harper's hair, and she playfully swatted him away, grinning. "Well, Ethan already warned her work needs to be limited while you're here. We all know your tendencies toward workaholism."

He threw up his hands. "Guilty as charged. But these two women will keep me in line."

Alyssa's cheeks heated at the pleasure his comment gave her. Since they'd arrived, she'd watched him soften and relax into the environment in a way she rarely glimpsed. She loved seeing the other side of him, hanging with his daughter, just being a dad rather than the mayor.

"I feel a bit guilty going riding when Ophelia is in the kitchen all day," Alyssa admitted. "I tried to help, but she and Kyle shooed me right out."

Harper winked. "Take my advice and stay out. Those two are experts when it comes to cooking, and Ophelia enjoys putting on a big spread for Turkey Day. Our time will come with the cleanup. That's bad enough."

Chloe wrinkled her nose. "Yeah, I saw a million pots and pans and trays in there that will all need washing. Kyle and Ethan always disappear around that time with some excuse."

"Your father is excellent at washing dishes," Alyssa said primly. "I'm sure he'll dive right in."

Jonathan's face fell. "I thought I was a guest."

Harper patted him on the shoulder. "Nah, you're family now. Aren't you lucky?"

A strange sound like a giggle burst from Alyssa's lips at the horror on his face. His gaze caught hers and softened, lingering a bit longer than it should. She swallowed back the ache in her throat and refocused on Chloe, who was speaking.

"Why don't you and Dad head to that barn and get acquainted with Flower and Bambi? They're already tacked up and ready. Carrots are on the shelf. I'll be right back."

Harper spoke up. "Have a good ride, guys. I'll meet you at the inn within the hour, and we can get ready to feast." They waved goodbye and watched as Phoenix and Captain Hoof followed her down the path and disappeared into the back barn.

Jonathan hesitated, glancing into the shadowed interior where the horses waited. "There's no, umm, surprises waiting inside, right?"

"Probably just Bolt and a few of his doggie pals," Chloe said. "On this farm, you never know what rescues you'll run into."

Jonathan snorted. "Goats and horses and dogs and cats are fine, as long as that mad chicken stays away."

"You scared of Hei-Hei, Dad?" Chloe asked with delight. "He's a sweetie, and Mia has full control of him."

"What chicken?" Alyssa asked. It was rare that Jonathan was wary of anything, let alone an animal.

Jonathan shuddered. "Trust me, you don't want to meet him. Besides being scary as hell, every time Mia and I try to work, he glares at me. And when Mia leaves me alone, he pecks at my foot like he's giving me a warning. I don't know how Ethan deals with him."

"He's just overprotective," Chloe said. "Give me ten minutes, and we'll be ready for our ride."

"Fine, but if Alyssa screams, someone better come and help," he muttered, leading the way. Chloe's laugh echoed in the air.

Flower and Bambi both had matching white coats, were average-size, and seemed gentle. Alyssa fed them carrots, and their teeth grasped them gingerly, rolling the vegetable around before settling into a rhythm of crunches. Flower leaned over and nibbled at her bun, which tickled, but her heart melted when she looked into those sweet brown eyes and saw the affection so freely given.

"Did you ever ride before Chloe came to the farm?" she asked curiously. Jonathan seemed confident with the horses, stroking Bambi's flank and talking sweet nothings into a pricked ear. Was it wrong that she was jealous of a horse? She tore her gaze away from those talented fingers and reminded herself he was giving her everything she asked.

No flirting. No touching. No intimacy.

It sucked, and it was only the beginning of the weekend.

"No, it wasn't something I was interested in. I was always more comfortable with city life and, other than a family dog, we never had much contact with animals. But watching Chloe change and grow made me want to share in her passions. This rescue farm is quite something. It used to be half the size it is now."

"Is it just me, or are most of the animals named for Disney characters?"

He shook his head in dismay. "No, they are. Seems the Bishop women grew up with Disney in the forefront, and now all their rescues are dubbed with character names. I don't know how the men live with this stuff."

"Chauvinism is not a quality worthy of the governor, Mr. Mayor," a voice rang out, strong and clear. Footsteps echoed behind them, and Alyssa turned. The woman who stood framed in the doorway had her arms crossed in front of her chest and a scowl on her lovely face. Her hair was a pretty honey color, cut sharply to angle under her chin. Amber eyes sparked with annoyance as she glared at Jonathan, her brows snapped together in a frown. She wore a black, stretchy dress that was clearly designer, and high-heeled leather boots with gold stacked heels. Under the trendy belt, her massive belly poked out. Alyssa pegged her at about seven months. Her polished appearance and fierce demeanor could both intimidate and charm, depending on the situation, and Alyssa admitted she'd always had a girl crush on Mia Thrush-Bishop, owner of Strategic Solutions PR, one of the most thriving firms in Manhattan. Jonathan was her client.

Jonathan winced. "Sorry, Mia. Guess Disney isn't my thing."

"Because you never sat down and watched a movie with us. I guess we'll have to change that tonight. I'll ask Chloe if we should pick *Cocoa* or her favorite, *Moana.*"

Jonathan rubbed his face with a groan, and she caught Mia's wink. "Please don't make me watch cartoons on one of my precious evenings off."

"Trust me, it'll be great PR. Slipping in a quote from a family movie for a sound bite will be gold for the voters."

"You are going to be the scariest mom on the planet."

She flashed him a dangerous smile. "Damn, I hope so." Mia walked over without even a waddle and gave Alyssa a big hug. "I was so excited when I heard you were coming. Been dying to get you out here. Happy Thanksgiving, babe."

Alyssa hugged her back, her throat closing up with emotion. Mia had always been an advocate and supporter, and they'd grown close. "How are you feeling? You look amazing."

Mia snorted, heading over to give Jonathan a matching hug. "I feel like a penguin. My body has become an alien pod, and I'm crossing off the days until the little one decides he or she has cooked enough."

"Not finding out if it's a boy or girl?" Jonathan asked.

"Nope, we want it to be a surprise. You going for a ride by

yourselves?"

"No, Chloe just had to do a few things, but she's taking us on the trail," Jonathan said. "Maybe we can carve out some time together tomorrow? I've already been warned no more than two hours of work for us."

"Damn, me, too." Mia sighed in frustration. "Ethan's become a bit cranky lately. It's like he's pregnant, too. He's freaking me out."

"Couvade Syndrome," Alyssa said. "It's a real condition where men experience all the symptoms of their partner's pregnancy. Has he experienced bouts of nausea, weight gain, or swelling? Cravings? Anxiety or stress regarding the birth?"

"All of it." Mia cooed and patted Flower and Bambi. "Thing is, Ethan never complains, but I've noticed weird stuff. He's suddenly eating tons of Ben & Jerry's ice cream, and he never liked it before. He puts his feet up at night, and his ankles are twice the size. And his research on this birth is crazy. I find website articles marked, printouts galore, books that I don't want to read scattered everywhere, all while he tries to drill me about the latest facts so I'm prepared. Ugh, like I'll ever be prepared for this, no matter what the research."

Jonathan laughed. "Poor bastard. He survived special-ops, a shooting, PTSD, and now it's the baby that finally beats him."

"Well, we're taking our full two hours for work, and he'll just have to deal."

"I believe you two can rule the world with two hours," Alyssa said.

Mia blew her a kiss. "We're going to try. Let me get back to the house. I'll see you in there. Remember, dinner's at four p.m."

She strode out without missing a beat. Alyssa glanced over to find Jonathan smiling. "You really care about her," she said softly. She loved that about him, the way he was fiercely loyal to the people close to him and protected them at all costs.

"She's special. Without her, Chloe and I may have never been this close. She had the guts to challenge me on my decisions like no one else, no matter how hard I fought her."

"You never had feelings for her?" she asked curiously. "Tried to date?"

His eyes widened, and he laughed long and hard, startling the horses. "Oh, hell, no. Mia and I would've been a disaster—we're both high-strung personalities. Plus, there was never any attraction. It's funny how everyone assumes a pretty face makes a man fall hard, but chemistry has always been the thing I've struggled with most. I fell hard for my wife in college and never looked at another woman. After she passed, the only woman I ever experienced that with was—" He stopped short, clearly realizing his mistake a bit too late.

Her name was never spoken aloud but hung in the air like smoke after a gunshot nonetheless.

"Sorry," he muttered, taking a step back as if he were afraid he might reach out and try to touch her.

Her whole body clenched then practically wept with the need to tell him she couldn't do this anymore. That she'd take a chance. That she wanted him badly, too, and it would all be worth the blow-up.

She opened her mouth, but a shadow fell over them, moving closer. Suddenly, his face changed.

"Don't move," he whispered. "Don't even breathe."

"Is it a bear?" she whispered back, scared to turn. "Sasquatch can't be in this area. It's not north enough."

"Worse. It's that damn chicken."

Slowly, she turned. Blinked. And studied the giant, monster fowl that stood a few feet away.

The thing had massive feet and claws, towering tall with a thick body of mottled black. Fat red jowls hung from under his beak. Crazy white feathers stuck out from his head like a designer hairdo gone terribly wrong. A high-pitched shriek emitted from him, and she watched in horror as he scraped his clawed foot on the ground like he was about to charge.

"Hei-Hei," Jonathan yelled. "Don't you dare! If you give me shit, I'll tell Mia, and you'll be on the table for Thanksgiving instead of under it!"

The chicken monster clearly didn't like that because he began to cluck and squawk, shaking out his feathers in fury and walking closer.

Alyssa wondered what death by chicken would feel like.

"Good boy," she whispered. "Pretty boy. Nice boy."

"Be gone, chicken from hell!" Jonathan boomed.

And then, Hei-Hei decided he'd had enough.

He charged toward Jonathan, ignoring Alyssa, and began to peck madly at the mayor's feet. Flower and Bambi barely gave him a glance as if used to his temper tantrums, and Jonathan began howling, trying to get away. And then—

"Hei-Hei!"

The female voice snapped out with pure authority. The chicken froze, whirling around, and came face-to-face with Mia. In a matter of seconds, the creature scurried away from Jonathan and began rubbing his feathers against Mia's boot-covered calf like a cat seeking to be petted.

"I am very disappointed in you," she said coolly. "I should have known you were trying to sneak into the barn. And here I was, about to share some special treats with you. Now I may give your portion to Captain Hoof."

The chicken pressed harder, making little sounds of what seemed like an apology. Alyssa stared in pure fascination at the obvious bond between them.

Mia sighed, and her face softened. "I'll think about it. Now, come with me and leave poor Jonathan alone. Ethan is going to be pissed you acted so badly with our guests." She shook her head. "Sorry, guys. He means well, he's just a tiny bit protective."

She left again, taking the chicken monster with her.

Alyssa glanced over. His face was a bit pale, and he seemed to lean against Bambi for comfort. "You okay?" she asked, pressing her lips together.

"Of course." He scoffed like the whole scene was nothing. "I wasn't afraid. I just didn't want him to hurt you. Are *you* okay?"

Mirth threatened, but she smothered it. The man needed to have some pride left. "Yes, thanks for helping me. He was definitely scary."

"No problem."

Chloe hurried in. "Sorry I'm late, had more to do than I thought. Did I miss anything?"

They shared a glance and, suddenly, they were both laughing together, and Alyssa knew this weekend was already going horribly wrong in the worst way possible.

She was falling even more in love with Jonathan Lake.

Chapter Nine

Jonathan bowed his head to say grace and tried not to feel anything when Alyssa's fingers tangled with his. As they asked for blessings and gave gratitude for the food on the table, and people to share it with, he wondered if he was really able to continue this way.

The past few weeks had been torturous. He kept believing it would get easier, but every night, he tossed and turned and dreamt about her. Trying to keep his emotions locked tightly away was more work than he'd imagined. Each time she came into his office, her scent teased him mercilessly. He tried to focus on her barrage of instructions and questions, but all he could think about was how she'd tasted. When she sat next to him at a meeting, her leg occasionally casually brushed his, and he'd needed to stay at the table longer than necessary so he didn't betray his weak body and painful erection.

But he wouldn't surrender. Alyssa was too important for him to lose, and he'd learn to deal with sheer grit and determination.

Still, this weekend wasn't easy. Seeing her at the farm showed him a glimpse of the woman she hid while at the office. She was more relaxed and open here, her gaze feasting on the sights around her with a happiness that touched him. Watching her ride Flower, her body moving well with the horse, her occasional laughter drifting in the cold breeze, made him realize he might be doomed to secretly love her forever. She'd chatted with Chloe easily, and he'd just listened, enjoying her obvious affection for his beloved daughter. Having the two most important women in his life flanking him as they rode down the trails with the mountains in the distance and the fading sun at his back was a moment he'd never forget.

He shook off his thoughts and refocused on the conversation at the table.

"Seems like Kyle has become the new Nicholas Sparks," Ethan said. "Who would've thought *A Brand New Ending* would rank as one of the best romance movies of the year? I went into town the other day, and Bea's granddaughter was home from college, gushing about how she saw the movie ten times and cried." His blue eyes glinted with amusement. "How does it feel being married to Mr. Romance, Tink?"

Ophelia shook her head at her brother's teasing and the familiar nickname permanently attached to her. Jonathan admitted she did look a little like the fairy with her blond hair, pointy chin, and huge, blue eyes. "I'm just happy he finally got a chance to write what he wants," she said, patting Kyle's hand. "Hollywood blocked him in so many ways, at least with LWW Enterprises, Presley lets him pitch his own stories. The next one is slated for next year, and I think it's even better."

Kyle's father, Patrick, sat at the other end of the table. He was a grizzly man with a soft spot for his rescue dog, Charlie. "I'm proud of you, son, but I still like those shoot 'em up movies. Maybe you can throw a car chase in the next one?"

Kyle grinned. "I hear you, Dad, but Ethan's really gonna love this one. It's based on a cool PR executive coming to a small B&B for the summer and falling for a moody, not-so-handsome hero with issues. Thing is, he's called the horse whisperer and seems to rehabilitate abused thoroughbreds. The one he works with ends up winning the Derby. Good stuff, huh?"

Ethan dropped his fork and stared at him. "Oh, hell no. You are not writing about me like some warped hero, or using ridiculous terms like the horse whisperer. That book's already been written."

"Not the way I'm gonna write it," Kyle said, the teasing threat made clear. "Get ready, buddy. You're about to be famous."

"Son of a bitch," he growled.

Mia squealed with delight. "You're writing our love story! That's amazing. Do I get to help screen the actress who'll play me?"

Harper laughed. "Probably not, but I'm sure Kyle will guarantee you're properly represented."

"Definitely," Kyle said. "I'm thinking Ethan should be played by Robert Redford. He's a bit old now, but he can pull you off."

Ethan glared. "Bullshit. Aidan, help me out here, buddy. He's going to be writing about you, too, and Phoenix. All we need is more press at our farm—I can't take it."

Aidan had his head down, shoveling in mashed potatoes and biscuits, but he looked up. With a heavy Irish brogue, he said, "Hmm, did you tell Kyle the bad news about Hei-Hei?"

Kyle looked nervous. "What about him?"

"Well, when the baby comes, Mia needs a quiet environment, and since Hei-Hei needs to stay indoors during the winter, you're going to have to take him in."

Horror widened the man's eyes. "Oh, hell, no. That chicken wants to kill me."

"Life's a bitch, ain't it?" Ethan drawled, punching Aidan in the shoulder with gratitude. "Thanks, Aidan. You were always my favorite brother-in-law."

Harper laughed. "All of you are nuts," she said, shaking her head. "Sorry, Alyssa, meals in this house get a bit lively. Chloe knows well."

"Yeah, I remember the first time Mia and I had dinner here. I was pissed because I thought she was having an affair with Dad."

Jonathan choked on a piece of turkey. He gulped some water and faced his daughter in shock. "You never told me that! Mia and I never had a relationship!"

Ethan shrugged. "I thought you two had a thing, also. Now I realize it's ridiculous. You'd kill one another."

"Chloe, I wish you would have asked me," Jonathan said.

His daughter gave him a gentle smile. "We had too many issues back then, Dad. Winning the election was priority, and I was pissed at the world. But my point was watching how far we've all come. Now, the table is double the size." She beamed, looking at the couples gathered around. "I think it's really cool. And now Alyssa is part of us."

Mia raised her glass of sparkling apple cider, her eyes gleaming with a bit of wetness. "Let's have a toast to that. To love, in all ways, for all of our days."

Ethan rested his hand on her belly and kissed her cheek. "I'll toast to that."

They clinked glasses, and Jonathan caught Alyssa's gaze, full of longing and regret, and a vulnerability that shredded his insides. She deserved all of it. A big, crazy family who loved her exactly as she was. A man to show her every day that she was special and beautiful and…everything.

Patrick cleared his throat. "Can we let the animals in now? Poor Charlie's been at Mia's with that awful chicken, and I promised him some turkey."

Ophelia sighed. "You know the rules are I never let animals in the house because of guests, but we're clear till Sunday, so I have a few days to do some deep cleaning."

"Is that a yes?" Harper asked hopefully.

"That's a yes. Go get the rest of your loved ones."

Patrick and Harper jumped up with Chloe and rushed out.

"Do you have any pets, Alyssa?" Ophelia asked with a smile.

"Not yet. But this weekend convinced me to get a cat. I'll ask Chloe for help. My hours are insane, so I need to be careful."

"That's smart, too many people get a puppy, then realize no one will be there all day. Did you have fun horseback riding?"

Her face lit up. "Yes, it was amazing. I never felt so free before. And being with the horses made me realize how special they are. It's like the only thing they want from you is to be loved—no rules, limits, or conditions. Wouldn't it be beautiful to be that brave? To love someone like that?"

A hush fell over the table. Jonathan fisted his hands, desperate to reach over and pull her into his arms. Bury his lips in her hair and show her how badly he wanted to give her that type of love.

Suddenly, he caught Mia's gaze across the table. She cocked her head, studying him with narrowed eyes.

She knew.

But he couldn't hide his emotions here, and right now, he didn't have to. Mia was a master at keeping secrets and respecting privacy. It was a miracle she hadn't figured it out before.

Ophelia sighed. "That's how everyone should be loved, at least once. But the way you expressed it was perfect. Maybe Kyle can use you for inspiration."

Kyle winked. "Got all the inspiration I need right here, baby," he said, giving her a kiss.

Ethan made gagging noises.

They laughed, and in minutes, the house exploded with a variety of canines, felines, fowl, and a goat. There were barks, and chicken shrieks, and bleats, and meows, as small plates of turkey were dispersed. Afterward, Alyssa and Chloe got on the floor and rubbed Charlie's belly, fussed over Figaro the beautiful black and white cat, and played with Captain Hoof.

"Dish duty," Kyle called out, rocking back and forth on his heels with glee. "Who's up?"

"I'll do it," Mia said, beginning to rise.

Ethan eased her back down. "Not you, sweetheart. Just relax."

Jonathan noticed her usual argument that pregnancy limited none of her skills seemed to disappear for the occasion. She made a grateful kissing sound and settled down with a triumphant expression.

Damn, she was good.

Patrick sighed with fake sorrow. "Really sorry, but my hands have been experiencing bad arthritis now. It'd be real painful for me. Must've been all those years of crackin' my knuckles."

"Oh, that's just a myth," Alyssa interrupted. "Cracking knuckles doesn't cause arthritis. The sound is simply gas bubbles bursting."

Patrick shot her a look. "Well, I still got bad arthritis and can't do dishes." Alyssa seemed to realize the high stakes of this game and quickly snapped her jaw shut. He tried not to laugh.

Kyle raised a brow. "Good one, Dad. Next?"

Aidan raised his hand. "I was training this new horse, and the bastard threw me. Now my back's a bit messed up."

Ethan snorted. "You're a champion trainer, and a colt threw you?"

"Yeah, it was terrible. Harper was terrified for me, weren't you, love?"

"Sure, Irish. Terrified."

Kyle nodded. "Not bad. Ethan?"

"Remember how I got shot a few years back? Well, you know how when the cold weather comes in, my knee hurts like a son of a bitch? I can barely stand. Don't think dishes would be a good idea."

Ophelia groaned and rolled her eyes. "Unbelievable. Not one of you feels guilty about sticking Jonathan with all those dishes, huh?"

He realized then that the guys didn't think he could bring it. The sheen of success was already carved on their faces, but they didn't know a man didn't get to be mayor without playing a few games of hardball. He swiped his hands together and spoke.

"Sorry, gentlemen, but I'll have to pass on dishes. I have a call with the president in about ten minutes."

Silence descended.

Alyssa's eyes sparkled with mirth, and Mia clamped her lips together as if trying desperately not to laugh.

The four men at the table stared at him with shock and begrudging respect.

Kyle inclined his head. "You win, Mr. Mayor. Gentlemen, the Brillo pads are under the sink with the extra sponges. Good luck. We're going to enjoy an after-dinner drink on the porch."

Kyle took his wife's hand and led her away from the mess of piles, leftovers, soiled pots and pans, and endless crystal glasses littered across the table.

Ethan shot him a glare. "You're good, dude," he muttered, then strode into the kitchen with a bit of a temper. Patrick cursed and then slowly followed, with Aidan trailing on his heels.

Mia winked. "And that's why you're going to be governor of New York."

Alyssa laughed.

It was the sweetest sound he'd ever heard.

And in that moment, Jonathan realized this was one of the best Thanksgivings he'd ever had.

* * * *

Alyssa sat outside in a comfortable rocker. The wraparound porch boasted various chairs, afghans, and a portable heater to keep guests warm on colder nights. After the kitchen had been cleaned, they feasted on dessert and settled down to watch *Moana*. She's seen it many times over the years with her parents—any type of movie was acceptable in their house—but watching it with a huge family, snuggled next to Jonathan and Chloe, had been magic.

She'd watched as he tried to pick a place across the room, but Chloe had dragged him over, pushing Alyssa right next to him on the giant sectional couch. Most of the movie, she desperately tried not to focus on the hard length of his leg pressed against hers, or his shoulder an inch away, or his carved profile flickering in shadow. His ocean scent teased her nostrils, and her tummy gave maddening flutters every time he turned to her and gave that sexy half-smile.

She was beginning to break apart piece by piece.

At the end, Chloe sang the song *You're Welcome* in her father's ear, and Alyssa watched them play-fight and giggle before settling into a long chat by the fireplace. She'd sought some alone time outside, giving them privacy.

The night was still, and she wrapped her arms around her knees as she stared into the darkness, enjoying the various sounds of the night creatures coming alive to play. The screen door shut, and Mia sank down into the rocking chair next to her.

"I love seeing them like that together," Mia commented. "He's changed a lot. Both of them have."

There were too many things she could say, and all would give away her heart. So she just nodded. "It's nice to see a close father/daughter relationship. He's sweet."

Mia seemed to still, cranking her head around to stare. "What did you say?"

"Jonathan. He's sweet."

Alyssa fought a blush at the woman's searing gaze, as if her inner secrets and soul had been dragged out and revealed. "Jonathan Lake is not sweet. He's stubborn, loyal, and a visionary. He's an amazing, supportive father. He's one of the best businessmen I've met. But girlfriend, he's not sweet."

Alyssa blinked, trying to extract herself from this without giving herself away. "Of course you're right. Not sure where that adjective sprang from."

Mia sighed. "Oh, babe, I think you know. You poor thing. You're in love with him."

Cheeks burning, cursing herself for acting juvenile when she barely broke a sweat in a room full of high-powered men barking at each other like the world depended on their next decision, she forced a laugh. "Don't be ridiculous. I've worked with the mayor for almost three years now. Sometimes people get the wrong idea."

Mia snorted. "I should have known something was going on. I've never seen Jonathan so happy. At first, I thought it was the run for governor, or being in a great place with Chloe, but I sensed something bigger. I can't believe I missed it during all those meetings we spent together. The way he looks at you when he thinks no one's watching. The way he smiles with his whole being when you hang with Chloe. He finally found the right woman after all this time. He found you."

"I'm not the right woman," she said automatically. "I'm not his type."

"You are exactly his type. Jonathan bores way too easily. With you, he'll be lucky if he ever knows what will happen next."

Enough. She couldn't stand another person misjudging who she was and thinking Jonathan and she were a perfect fit. "Listen to me! I may be good at my job, but when I'm done, I want to be home. Alone with my books and music and TV. I don't even have an animal, that's how isolated I like to be. I hate people. I am not even close to being suited for that man."

"Why?" Mia asked curiously. "What type of man do you really think he is?"

"He's dynamic and opinionated and larger than life. He runs a city, and soon, he'll run a state. He loves being around people, and at the top of his game. He's an adventurer. After a month of living together, he'd realize how boring I really am."

Mia's face gentled, and she reached out to grasp Alyssa's hand. She startled at the intimate, supportive touch, not understanding what was about to happen. She'd rarely had many friends throughout her life. "Babe, I'm so sorry. I didn't realize how scared you are. Boy, I don't blame you. I fricking freaked out when Ethan and I were falling for each other, and we had a lot of obstacles to work on, but I need you to hear this and truly listen to me. I've known Jonathan for a long time, and I've never seen him look at a woman the way he looks at you. He's at peace. He smiles. His energy is different. You've worked for him for a while, do you really think he doesn't realize who you are? You're using the image of him to protect yourself because then you won't get hurt. Pretty typical stuff, right off the therapist's couch."

Alyssa sifted through every word, trying to dig deep and see if there was any truth to it. "My main concern is his career, Mia. You know, you're his publicist. He doesn't need any scandal, and sex with his assistant constitutes a problem. The press will be all over it. I can't let our relationship cost him the election."

Mia cocked her head and frowned. "He's widowed, and it's been five years. He's allowed to date, even in the public eye. I think it may even boost his image. Women secretly worry he's a big player behind the scenes."

Alyssa took off her glasses and rubbed her eyes. Frustration simmered. "I'm his executive assistant. I accompany him to all public functions. I run his office and calendar. I'm with him behind most closed-door meetings. With the #metoo movement in full swing, he could catch a lot of heat, and we can't risk it."

Mia tapped her finger against her lip, considering. "I see your point, but it has nothing to do with #metoo because he never pressured you, discriminated against, or did things you didn't want. You both chose, as grown adults, to dive into a relationship. Will it be easy? Hell, no. Can we make it work? Yes. Because I know how to spin everything. I have boots on the ground, contacts at all papers, and on social media sites. If we get ahead of it before there are any leaks, I can perform magic." Her attitude should have been smug, but it was all kick-ass confidence. Alyssa's respect for Mia went up a thousand notches. She loved a woman who knew she was good at her job and not afraid to tell the world. Too many women had learned along the way to soften their successes, explain things away, making it easy for the outside world to steal their power.

No more. No woman should feel ashamed to own her talents. She saw the same fire in Chloe, an assurance that she could do anything with enough work and determination. It was special, and unfortunately, still too rare. But she was hopeful the next generation would follow the path through.

"Unless something else is holding you back." Mia peered into her face as if digging for the real truth. Then her golden eyes softened with sympathy Alyssa didn't understand. "Oh, I get it. It's not really about Jonathan or the election. It's about you."

She gasped. "Excuse me? This has nothing to do with me, other than putting my career at risk, which I don't want to lose."

"No, believe me, I know how difficult it'd be, but I've seen Jonathan fight for something he wants, and he's fierce. Protective. He'll do what needs to be done, and so will I. But this is about you not wanting to be in the spotlight. I don't blame you, Alyssa. A political partner is a bitch to deal with, so it's better if you realize you can't handle it now before you break his heart."

Her jaw dropped. "Me, break his heart? I'm doing this to protect him because I care. I couldn't live with myself if he lost the election because of a sex scandal with his office partner."

"It's not about sex, it's about love. A relationship. You'll date in the public eye. We'll make an announcement, control how we want the world to find out, and deal with some fallout. Mostly, I think it'll be great for ratings. But you will have a hard time." Her voice strengthened. "You need to believe in yourself and him and know you can stand together even when it's tough. I'm crazy about you, Alyssa. I think you were meant to be with Jonathan, but maybe that's just not a life you can handle."

The words were vicious, tearing at her like tiny, sharp jabs that drew blood. She caught her breath, but Mia kept her direct stare, and she realized she wasn't trying to be mean. She was just telling the truth.

Dear God, she was right.

All this time, her real fear was being dragged out into the public eye and mocked. Just like she'd spent her entire life dealing with parents who poked and jabbed and tried to get her to be an actress when all she wanted to do was sit with her books. Pushed her into the spotlight in large groups of people, waiting for her to perform, whether it be conversation, a joke, or an interesting anecdote. All until she ventured deep inside herself where she couldn't be reached or hurt. She'd sought out assistant positions her entire life, comfortable in the role, enjoying working behind the scenes to reach perfection. It was where she excelled. But this would mean stepping out into a whole different role.

The mayor's girlfriend.

The realization slammed hard, throwing her into doubt. She'd been spinning excuses to keep Jonathan away, citing everything but her own secret fear.

Could she handle a life in the public eye with this man?

Or was it too high of a price to pay?

"Oh, Alyssa, I'm sorry. I didn't say that to hurt you. I think it's good to be honest, and Jonathan deserves it. So do you. Can I help in any way?"

Still bruised, Alyssa shook her head and forced a smile. "No. I'm not mad. You're right. I just didn't realize it." She nibbled at her lip and slipped her glasses back on. "I have to think."

"Just remember, love doesn't really add up nicely on a ledger. It's messy and damn scary. It's like jumping off a cliff, and you have a fifty/fifty shot of either dying or flying. Some risk the cliff over and over. Others figure their statistics are crappy, and they're better off walking than flying."

The image stuck in her head in crystal-clear clarity, blinding her with the sudden knowledge of what she'd been doing. "Yes, that makes perfect sense."

Mia reached over and gave her a half-hug, her belly blocking most of the contact. "Once you decide if he's worth it, don't look back. Just leap. Trust me, it seems to work best that way. Harper and Ophelia would agree with me."

"Thanks, Mia. I'm going to head to my room for a bit. Take some time."

She left the porch, already sensing change in the air, and a big decision to make.

To jump off the cliff or not.

It was a question she needed to answer.

Chapter Ten

Jonathan followed the pathway toward the barns, letting the light of the moon guide his way. He'd tossed and turned for a while before giving up on sleep. It was impossible, knowing Alyssa was right next door. He imagined her naked, hair loose over the pillow, eyes sleepy without the protection of her glasses, arms reaching out for him.

Yeah, after a cold shower, he'd decided to get some air. The inn was quiet, and he enjoyed the cover of darkness for both his body and heart, which ached with the knowledge that he'd never be able to have the only woman he wanted.

Being surrounded by family and friends for the holiday reminded him his job was an important part of him, but not everything. He'd been neglecting the man inside, who now craved a partner to share the high and low moments of his life with.

Would Alyssa be willing to wait until after the election? If he settled into the role of governor, maybe they'd have a chance. Control the press by bringing the announcement to the public, or at least easing them in. It wasn't like he was having an affair or betraying his late wife. Mia could spin it as a positive experience—the well-known bachelor finally settling down into domestic bliss.

His thoughts spun with possibilities, but the whisper came deep from his gut.

Her life will change forever. She'll always be in the public eye. Is that what she really wants?

Probably not.

He reached the barns, the interiors dimly lit, but he knew the security cameras were whirring. Ethan was a former bodyguard and made sure his property and the people he loved were well protected. It was another reason Jonathan never worried when Chloe spent time here.

He made his way toward the back and sat on a large rock, his gaze studying the shadowy outline of mountains. Hundreds of stars winked brightly from the velvety sky. The wind rushed past his face, icy cold but refreshing, and he sat with his thoughts and the quiet for a while.

A twig cracked behind him.

He stiffened, wondering about large animals other than sweet rescues, but his body recognized her like a mate. Slowly, he turned.

She stood behind him, her arms clasped tightly across her chest. Her ash-blond hair was loose and fell like a waterfall of silk past her shoulders. She wore jeans, old sneakers, and a black wool coat. Her nose was pink in the chilly air.

"Are you okay?" he asked, shifting his weight to look at her fully. "What are you doing out here, Alyssa?"

Her chin tilted up a few notches. "Same as you, I imagine. Couldn't sleep." She moved closer, and his body automatically tensed, battling the need to touch her. "What are you thinking about?"

You. Always you.

"Work, of course." He paused. "Did you have fun today?"

"It was the best Thanksgiving I ever had."

The simple words tore at him. She was a woman who deserved so much love. But he also realized life was a choice. She didn't have to be lonely. She just had to choose to be with people she cared about instead of being alone. God, how he wanted to give her that.

He wanted to give her everything.

Slowly, he uncurled himself from his seated position and faced her. Moonlight bathed her profile, coating her skin in a silvery glow. Her big, brown eyes were trained on him, glinting with an odd intensity and determination he didn't understand. "Why?" he asked softly. "Because you were with Chloe? And friends? With people who care? It should be that way all the time, you know. Maybe you need to start asking for more in your life."

He waited for a defensive comment, or for her to step back and retreat. Instead, she moved closer, and the air shimmered with anticipation and electricity. "All of it. But mostly because I was with you."

"We were together last year at the soup kitchen."

A sigh spilled from her lips. "It was different then. I hadn't allowed myself to fall for you yet."

His heart slammed against his chest, and his nerves stretched thin, wondering what she was trying to say. "I promised you'd be safe here," he ground out. "From me. But God help me, Alyssa, tonight I'm just a man, and I want you. Go back to your warm bed, close the door, and tomorrow morning, we'll be back to what you want. We'll just be boss and employee. We'll be friends who respect and care about each other."

Her lower lip trembled but she didn't budge. "I've been thinking lately. About us, and all the reasons I've been scared to jump off the cliff with you. And I've realized it's more about me than you or the election. I'm scared of things I can't control. I always have been."

He fisted his hands to stop from reaching out and touching her. "We all are, sweetheart." The endearment slipped past his lips. "I don't blame you for not wanting this type of life. I want you to be happy."

"I know. Thing is, I'm beginning to realize I'm happiest with you. Ever since you opened the door and showed me more, I can't go back."

He stilled, his gaze delving deep. "What are you saying?"

"I'm saying I'm tired of being a coward. Of being safe. Of having an orderly, controlled, sterile life. I'm saying I want you."

A shudder wracked him. "And the election?"

A tiny shrug. "Mia's a master at her job for a reason. I'm willing to risk it if you are."

The admission crumpled him and the rest of his defenses. The primitive inside of him roared with satisfaction, desperate to get his hands on her body, imprint himself on her so deeply she'd never regret taking the chance. A growl rose from his chest, low and guttural.

"Then you need to come to me, Alyssa. I swore to keep my distance and not pressure you. This has to be about you and your choice."

Her eyes widened with recognition. His breath stalled out, and he wondered if she'd change her mind. If she'd step back and run from the intensity and mess before her, the choice to involve herself with a man endlessly in the public eye, who'd change her life forever.

She took the final steps. Slowly reached up and looped her arms around his neck. Her fingers cupped the back of his head and pressed it down so his lips hovered an inch from hers. He savored the sweet rush of her breath, the plump curve of her mouth, the slight tremble of her body as her breasts crushed his chest, and her hips arched up.

"I choose you," she whispered.

Then she pressed her lips to his.

The taste of her made him crazed. He took the kiss deep, plunging his tongue inside her mouth to conquer and pleasure and claim. She gave it all back, the sting of her nails in his back, the wildness stirring between them, hinting at the storm to come. He drank from her lips with greed, his hands cupping her face to hold her still, then nipped at her bottom lip.

"There are cameras out here," he said. "We can go back to the inn."

She shook her head, clinging tight. "No, can't wait. Plus, our rooms are too close together. Here."

He blistered out a curse. "Come with me." She gripped his hand, and he led her to one of the barns Chloe had shown him was used for storage. This one wasn't locked, and he slid the door shut behind him. The musty scent of hay and feed filled the air, and the space was stuffed with equipment and bags, dark except for the moonlight flooding through the lone window. He led her to the back where an old table sat beneath the windowsill and quickly stripped off her jacket, tugging off his clothes in a rushed frenzy, their fingers awkward in their zeal to finally be skin-to-skin.

"You deserve a bed," he ground out, bending his head to suck on a tight nipple, savoring the hoarse moans emitting from her throat. "You deserve hours of me worshipping you. You deserve a thousand orgasms."

She ripped off her glasses, wriggled her jeans down over her hips, and opened herself up for him, reaching to cup his throbbing erection. "Right now, the only thing I want is you inside of me—on this table— right here and right now—"

He groaned, thrusting into her greedy fingers, savoring the sleek feel of her soft skin and the spicy scent of her arousal. He moved her panties aside and inserted one finger into her dripping heat. She whispered his name urgently, and he added another digit, stretching her while one thumb tapped gently at her swollen clit, making sure she was ready.

He fumbled for the condom, sheathing himself with clumsy movements, then lifted her onto the table. She spread her thighs, and for one endless, perfect moment, he memorized her body in the moonlight, flushed and damp, quivering for him, open to anything he wanted to do. Humbled by the gift of her body and trust, he lowered his head and pressed a gentle kiss to her lips. Hooked his hands under her knees and lifted up.

Then plunged inside of her with one strong push.

* * * *

She was dying.

Alyssa was burning up, every inch of her desperate to soothe the fire on her skin and inside her body. From the moment she'd seen him alone, gazing at the stars, she realized this man deserved a woman willing to fight for him. To stand beside him, hold his hand, and face the future with bravery. There were never guarantees, and she was exhausted from trying to fight her heart. Jonathan Lake was meant to be hers.

It was finally time to claim him.

His lips were like wispy, gossamer touches over her lips, barely giving pressure, and his dick was buried deep inside her, invading every inch of her body with a fierce demand she give him everything. She fought for breath as she adjusted to his girth, the pressure a delicious mix of pain and pleasure, and then with a sigh, she opened completely, letting him in. He sank even deeper, and she shuddered, biting the meaty muscle in his shoulder. His fingers tightened on her hips.

"Alyssa."

Her name floated above her as if she were in a drunken haze, and she focused her gaze on the piercing, blinding blue that claimed her just as possessively as his body.

"Look at me, sweetheart. I need to see you when you're mine."

The masculine demand caused another rush of wetness, her inner muscles squeezing around him. He groaned with satisfaction, pressing deeper, his mouth brushing hers with excruciating gentleness. The contradiction of his hard thrusts taking her body was an intoxicating combination. She lifted herself up, the delicious scrape against her clit pushing her toward orgasm, and hung on while he fucked her and cherished her and made love to her on the battered old table in the musty barn.

She cried out his name when the orgasm rushed over her, jolting her like a shock of electricity. His muscles tightened, and he took the kiss deep, moaning into her mouth as he joined her. They clung together, slick with sweat, her muscles deliciously achy. She didn't notice her face was damp until his thumb brushed against her right cheek.

"Sweetheart, are you okay? Did I hurt you?"

She blinked, focusing on his worried face. "No."

"You're crying."

She took his fingers and pressed them to her lips. He was still deep inside her, and Alyssa realized at this moment, she fell utterly and irrevocably in love with the mayor.

Her mayor.

She smiled. "When a person cries, the first drop of tears from the left eye is pain. If it's from the right, it's happiness."

He smiled back, leaning his forehead against hers. His blue eyes lit with satisfaction and happiness filled her from the inside.

"Good to know. How about I take you back to my room?"

"No," she whispered. "I want to stay right here with you tonight. Is that okay?"

"Yeah, I think we can work something out."

They made a makeshift bed with a pile of bags, fresh hay, and a blanket. He wrapped his arms around her, and she closed her eyes and savored the last few hours of darkness.

* * * *

They drifted to sleep for a bit, and when he woke, he studied her face in the shadows. Her lips held the touch of a secret smile, and her blond hair spilled around her like a frame enhancing a beautiful painting. Her fair skin was flushed and scratched red in some places where his five o'clock shadow had rubbed. Her full breasts lifted with each breath, and her nipples were still hard from the chill in the air. She slept with abandon, the same way she gave her body—wholly and deeply, surrendering in a way she sometimes struggled with in the light of day.

He'd always enjoyed sex but found he needed a deeper connection to truly let go. The few short affairs he'd had since Catherine's death were pure physical itch and never scratched the surface. Now, as he stared down at Alyssa, he knew his entire being was cracked open. The orgasm had reached every inch of his body, dug into his soul, and allowed him to experience an ecstasy he'd only found with his wife.

Somehow, he'd been blessed with a second chance at love. He wanted to steep himself in it, to lock them in this barn for the next seven days so he could spend every minute learning every last secret.

She gave a tiny snort and shuddered as if knowing his thoughts. He couldn't help his hand from reaching out and trailing his fingers down the valley of her breasts, caressing her stomach and the crease at her hip. Her skin grew warm, and her body softened under his touch, even in sleep. A satisfied grin curved his lips, and he lowered his head.

There were some other places he wanted to brand his five o'clock shadow on.

His tongue licked a path downward, exploring her damp inner thighs, the swollen nub of her clit, the hot wetness of her pussy. Pushing her legs apart, he settled his shoulders between her spread thighs and learned that sweet, secret part of her, hidden behind a small patch of tight curls.

When she woke up moaning his name, he began to suck and lick, parting her with his thumbs. Her hips rolled and jerked under his ministrations. Her hands grabbed at his shoulders, her heels dug in, and he ran the flat of his tongue over her hard nub, plunging his fingers deep into her channel.

She came against his mouth with a wild abandon that made him feel like Superman himself, and he eased up on the pressure, kissing her with gentle humbleness that poured through him in waves.

Slowly, he lifted his head and slid back up her body.

Her drunken gaze locked on his.

"Did you know that other than humans, wolves, bears, and bats also perform oral sex?"

He blinked then began to laugh, long and deep and hard. The final knowledge slammed through him, and he couldn't hold back the confession he'd known for a long, long time.

"I love you, Alyssa Block."

He kissed her, and she kissed him back, threading her fingers through his hair.

"I love you, too, Jonathan Lake."

Chapter Eleven

Alyssa couldn't stop smiling.

The goofy grin and girlish need to be close was an odd experience. They'd woken up on Friday wrapped around each other, naked, chilly, and sore from trying to sleep on hay and feed bags. Giggling like naughty teens, they'd snuck back to their respective rooms at the inn, then tried hard not to make googly eyes at each other over breakfast.

Mia noticed it all, giving Alyssa a wink.

They rode horses and visited the local craft fair, where she picked up a dried floral wreath, blown-glass wine goblets, and an intricate wood carving of a horse that looked like Phoenix. Chloe bought a bag of warm apple cider donuts, and they feasted as they sampled craft beer from the local breweries. By the time they arrived back at the inn, she felt tipsy, but already knew it had nothing to do with the alcohol.

"I'm exhausted," Ethan said, stretching his back. "How about we all recess for a nap?"

Chloe groaned. "Come on, Ethan, even Mia's not tired. Sometimes I think you're the one who's pregnant!"

Mia laughed. Ethan glared. "Not cool, Chloe. I'm still recovering from doing one hundred pots and pans from yesterday."

"I should probably do a few rounds at the barn," Harper said. "You can come with me, Chloe."

Aidan took that moment to snatch her up and lift her into his arms like she was a fragile butterfly. "Don't think so, love. We're overdue for a nap. Catch you guys later."

Harper gasped. "What are you doing!"

"Making you rest. It's a holiday weekend, and I want a...nap."

Harper's cheeks turned red. "Oh."

He strode away with his wife in his arms, making Alyssa swoon a tiny bit. Chloe sighed. "Okay, I'm going to make a few phone calls, but don't forget, we're doing game night. Poker is first."

Kyle rubbed his hands together. "Good, I'm ready to redeem myself this round. But let me finish this chapter so I get my next advance check and can bet big."

Ophelia and Kyle disappeared. Mia shared a look with Jonathan. "Want to use our two-hour window and get some work done?" she asked him.

"Sounds good. That okay, Ethan?"

Ethan looked sorrowful. "No nap, huh?"

Mia pressed a kiss to his cheek. "We'll go to bed early instead."

He grumbled a bit, but Alyssa could tell it was just for show. "I'll check on the animals and do a few things at the house. Meet you back here for poker. Don't work too hard."

"Let me just grab my laptop," Mia said.

They were left alone on the front porch. Jonathan crooked his finger. "Come here, sweetheart."

She never hesitated. He enfolded her in his arms, hugging her tight, and she clung to his warmth and strength, sinking into him. They stayed like that for a while, and she tucked her head against his chest, enjoying the moment.

"I want to tell Chloe about us today," he whispered in her ear. "What do you think?"

"Definitely. You don't think she'll have a problem with it?"

"I think the opposite. She's going to be thrilled. She's dropped hints to me before about you, you know. I think she always secretly hoped we'd get together."

"What about when we get back?"

He pulled slightly away and stared down at her. His ocean-blue eyes were serious. "What do you want to do, Alyssa? I don't want to drag you into the spotlight in a messy way. Why don't we talk to Mia and figure out the best plan?"

"I think that's a good idea."

The sound of footsteps echoed down the path. They eased away from each other and watched one of Ethan's bodyguards make his way toward them.

"Mr. Mayor, we have a problem."

With a sinking heart, Alyssa realized their idyllic retreat was officially over.

* * * *

"Son of a bitch."

He stared at the picture of him and Alyssa in a tight embrace. The slant of their bodies and angled heads clearly showed an intimacy that was more than friendship. Definitely more than boss and employee. It was an announcement to the world that they were lovers.

He gritted his teeth and tried to remain calm. Diana Delaney looked at him with a touch of sympathy. "I'm sorry, Mr. Mayor, but I'm running the photo."

They'd met in a deserted parking lot in his car to talk. Once Ethan's bodyguard outed the photographer, he'd gone after her, but the damage had already been done. Even with tight security, Diana had figured out where he was and who'd he be with.

"Privacy means nothing to you, does it?" he bit out, not able to control the anger and fear rising up within him. Damnit, they'd just gotten together. He needed enough time to control the announcement so they didn't rip him to shreds. But this picture was about to ruin it all.

She shrugged. "There's no privacy for a public official," she said. "Part of the bargain."

"There's no scandal here to capitalize on. I'm a free man, allowed to date and see who I want."

"Then this shouldn't be a problem. Do you have a quote for me?"

"No."

"Does Alyssa Block want to comment? She's been your assistant for over two years now, right? How long have you been hiding your relationship?"

"No comment," he said. "Who tipped you off?"

"It doesn't matter. I won't reveal my sources."

He knew for certain there was no one suspicious of his relationship with Alyssa except for one person.

Whitney. The socialite would have loved to blow this up and punish Alyssa, especially after not taking her bribe. It had her fingerprints all over it.

But did it matter at this point?

"When are you going to print?"

"Tomorrow morning. Mr. Mayor, give me the story to accompany the photograph, and I may be able to help."

"There's nothing I can say to stop or delay this from running?"

He knew the answer before she said it anyway. Again, he might hate the way his privacy was eroded, and how the game was played, but he agreed it was all part of the life for an elected official. He had no choice.

But Alyssa did.

"Do what you have to, Diana. I'll do the same."

She nodded and left. Jonathan drove back to the inn. He had limited time to decide on the plan, but he needed to talk to Alyssa. Last night, they'd confessed their true feelings, but never spoke about what course to take when they returned to reality. Would she pull back from him? Change her mind about walking this path after her photo had been splashed all over the gossip rags? Would this type of life eventually rip them apart?

The questions whirled through his mind. He pulled up and found Mia on the porch, waiting for him. "Where's Alyssa?" he asked.

"Upstairs with Chloe. I think they're having a heart-to-heart. How bad is it?"

He rubbed his head and climbed the steps. "Bad. She's running a picture of Alyssa and me."

"Were you naked?"

He groaned. "No, we were hugging."

Mia chewed on her bottom lip. "Can it be spun?"

"No, it's obvious we're intimate."

"Then we go big. Blow it up ourselves. Shout it to the world. You don't want to be in the literal closet anymore, Jonathan. I say we take the risk, and you both tell the public to stick it. I just got off the phone with Bob, and he agrees completely."

He sank into the chair beside her. "That's a pretty big risk, Mia. I don't know if Alyssa is ready for something like this so soon." He muttered a curse. "Damnit, if I only had more time. We had a plan."

"Well, in politics and social media, we always need a plan A, B, and C. When does it run?"

"Tomorrow morning."

"With a story? Did you give her a comment?"

"No."

"Good. We'll do our own piece."

"Mia, I don't know if this is going to work."

"I'm a master, I thought you had more faith in me. And no one screws with Bob, he's a magician."

He shook his head. "Not you or Bob. Alyssa. I don't know if she can handle this with me."

The words made his gut clench, but admitting his fear to Mia eased some of the tension. She gave a sigh and reached over, taking his hand. "I get it. I had a talk with her yesterday because it was obvious you two were gaga over each other. It's not an easy life you're offering, Jonathan, but I think with you at her side, she can handle anything. She's stronger than she thinks."

He gave a half-laugh. "You can't help who you love, can you?"

Her face softened. "Nope. But that's why life is never boring. It gives us these tiny surprises that make all the hard stuff worth it."

"She's worth everything."

She smiled at him and squeezed his hand. "I bet she feels the same way about you. Why don't you go find out?"

He nodded, then went to find Alyssa.

* * * *

"You're in love with my dad?"

Her heart beat frantically against her chest, but Alyssa held her gaze. She prayed the slight shock would pass and be replaced by happiness, but she had to prepare for the worst. Chloe had lost her mother—the great love of her life—and she might still be possessive over sharing Jonathan with anyone.

But Alyssa knew she had one course left. She loved the man with her heart and soul, and his passion was politics. So was hers. She could stop being so damn afraid and step into the spotlight, standing beside him, or she could break it off and scramble back to her hiding place.

She was tired of being alone. This weekend had taught her about family and friends and how relationships made her feel strong. Why should she settle for anything less than a great love—no matter what the obstacles?

"Yeah, I am. I have been for a while, but it took me time to come to terms. Plus, it was confusing because we were working together, and your dad and I always respected our professional relationship. He was going to tell you, but I feel woman to woman, you deserve to know how I feel directly from me."

She didn't want to overstep, but it was important for Chloe to hear it from her.

A gamut of emotions flickered over the young girl's face. Then a slow smile spread across her lips, and she let out a sound of joy. "I knew it! Dad always acted different with you, and he's been so stubborn about dating, I should have suspected. I'm so happy, Alyssa. I couldn't have found someone better for Dad to love."

Emotion choked her throat as Chloe hugged her, and tears burned her eyes. Sweet relief poured through her body. "Thank you," she whispered. "That means everything to me. I'm pretty much just as crazy about you."

Chloe laughed and wiped at her eyes. "Ditto. What are you going to do? Announce it to the press? Keep it quiet for a while?"

She sighed. "Your dad just found out a picture was taken of us on the farm. I think it's going to be leaked to the press."

"What? Damn those vultures. We had a tight team trying to keep this weekend private!"

"I know, but this is something we'll be struggling with, especially when he becomes governor. We just have to deal with it."

"Mia will know what to do," Chloe said confidently. "Let's go talk to her."

"We will, but first, I have to check in with your dad. He was going to meet with the photographer to see if he could squash it first."

A tap on the door interrupted them. Jonathan stepped in, his face weary, and offered a tired smile. "Hey, ladies. Chloe, do you think I can speak to Alyssa for a few minutes alone?"

"Sure, Dad."

Alyssa stood from the bed to face him. The door shut quietly, and he began to pace. She wished she had an extra stress ball to toss him. "It was Diana. The picture shows us hugging, but it's pretty obvious we have feelings for each other. Mia had an idea, but it's a risk. She wants to announce it to the public on our own and hold a press conference. Get ahead of it. Bob agrees with that plan. But there's another choice."

"What?"

He avoided her gaze. "We can deny. Say we've been close friends—like family—and I was comforting you. There's still time for you to decide, Alyssa. The reality is, my life is lived in the spotlight. I know we can work within those borders to carve out private time, and once the buzz dies down, the press will move on to another story. Do I think you'll take some heat on the job? Yeah, I'm not going to lie. But I'll back you up, and we have a hell of a team that will support us, who doesn't give a crap that we're personally involved."

Everything inside of her stilled. An awful fear gripped her insides and took hold. Did he want to go back to the way things were? Had all of her protests finally taken hold, so he doubted she had the strength to be his partner? Did he regret saying he loved her last night?

Her throat dried up, but she pushed the words out. "Are you saying you want to deny our relationship?"

He stopped pacing. His piercing blue gaze locked with hers, and in those jeweled depths, she saw the truth. There was male temper there. Regret. Determination.

And love.

"Hell, no. But I love you, and I understand if this is too much. I'm saying I can still find a way out because if we go down this road, it's going to be messy. I need to know you're prepared and want to do it. I need to know—"

His voice broke off. Hope tore at her at the naked vulnerability carved on his features. "Need to know what, Jonathan?" she asked softly.

"I need to know if you think I'm worth this."

Her heart shattered. She knew years later, she'd pin this moment as the one that'd changed her life. In the barn, they'd made love, declaring their emotions privately to each other. But announcing it to the world in the bright glare of day was a leap of faith, trust, a declaration that forced them both to make a choice.

God, she was so happy he'd waited for her.

"Did you ever read *The Symposium* by Plato?" she asked.

He blinked. "Umm, yeah. In college. Not that I remember much."

"Plato asserts that all humans began as whole, hermaphroditic beings with four hands, four legs, four ears, and two identical faces on one head. A strange fusion of male and female. And these beings were quite powerful. Did you know that?"

He cocked his head, suddenly listening intently. "No. Go on."

"Well, they attacked the gods, so Zeus decided to humble these beings without completely destroying them. He split them in two—men and women. And in doing so, he created the desire of human beings to endlessly search for the other half of themselves in order to feel whole again. Finding that other part of yourself is love."

Slowly, she crossed the room and stood in front of him. She tipped her head back and reached out, her palm cupping his hard cheek. "You're the one who makes me feel whole. And I don't intend to give that up for anything."

A heartbreaking smile curved his lips, and then he was leaning down and kissing her, holding her tight against him. "I'm crazy about you, Alyssa Block. And I can't wait to stand in front of those cameras and declare you as my partner in all ways."

"I spoke with Chloe and told her I loved you," she said in between kisses. "She's thrilled."

"Told you. Now, let's get to Mia and plan our strategy to take on the world."

"Let's start with New York State and work our way up."

He pressed his forehead to hers and laughed, and she laughed with him.

Epilogue

One year later

She raised her champagne glass and tipped it to his. The slight clink had a merry sound that went perfectly with the roaring fire in the background. After endless parties, crowds, and excited meetings for the past few days, it was nice to finally enjoy some quiet time to truly celebrate.

Jonathan Lake was now the newly elected governor of New York.

She studied his bare-chested form, sprawled out on the rug in front of the fireplace. Hair tousled, gleaming blue-black in the flickering light, golden skin stretched over glorious muscles. He was propped up on his elbow, a satisfied grin on his face. Her belly dipped, and once again, she had to remind herself that he was all hers. Every delicious, masculine inch of him.

"Have I told you lately I think you're hot?" she asked curiously.

A low laugh rumbled in his chest. Her gaze raked over tight abs and the dark line that arrowed straight down to disappear under his jeans. She'd never thought of herself as a sexual person, but when he was near, her body practically lit up on command.

All the time.

"I think you showed me perfectly last night," he drawled, those ocean-blue eyes glinting with hunger. "But we can do it again."

She smiled and lay down next to him, taking his hand. "Nope, you do the work tonight. I'm exhausted."

He laughed and pressed a kiss to her lips. "Me, too. Been a hell of a week."

"Hell of a year. But we did it." She stroked his cheek. "Not without some mishaps, but I knew we'd get to this point."

"You always believed in me," he said softly. "Even from the beginning."

"Because I always knew the type of man you were. New York is lucky to have you, Mr. Governor. I spoke with Chloe—I told her we'd be at the farm for Thanksgiving again."

"Good. I can spend Wednesday at the soup kitchen. Want to join me?"

"Of course." They sipped their champagne, and Alyssa savored the quiet. It had been touch and go for a while after they announced their relationship to the press, but Mia and her team had spun every story to emphasize a growing love between them that couldn't be denied any longer. Television ate it up, and though they had some pushback from some women believing Jonathan had used his position to force a romance, the majority of the voters came out in droves to support. She'd taken some coaching classes from Mia on dealing with the press better and gained confidence as the months passed and she dove into the election run. In the end, Alyssa had proven to herself that she was stronger than she believed and could hold her own in the public eye.

Chloe had blossomed into the new hot topic when she made an announcement defending their romance, stating that her father deserved a woman to love again. She was dubbed the darling of the press, attractive and passionate on issues, just like her father, and now had to deal with the spotlight. Jonathan hated it, but she'd watched Chloe grow this past year into a woman of her own.

It was too bad Owen was still a sore spot, but Alyssa was hopeful she'd finally meet a man to help her move on.

"Are you ready for our next challenge?" he asked, snagging her wrist and pressing a kiss to her palm.

"Of course. You were meant to be governor, and I can't wait to help you."

"Not talking about that. Talking about being my wife." Her ring flashed, a simple emerald cut that was elegant but not overwhelming. She was guilty of peeking at it constantly throughout the day, the symbol of a new life for them.

"Got it covered. Chloe and Mia will help me with the planning. We should delay a honeymoon until you're settled in first."

He nipped at her palm, then swiped his tongue across the sensitive flesh. She shivered. "Did you know everyone has a unique tongue print just like fingerprints?"

He put the glass down and slowly pushed her onto her back. A sexy smile settled on his lips. "No, but did you know the clitoris has eight thousand nerve fibers to help a woman achieve orgasm?"

She blinked. "That many, huh?"

He laughed, sliding his leg between her thighs. "Yep. Some facts need testing, though." He lowered his head, and she moaned, her body melting under his touch.

Much later, she collapsed beside him, boneless. He'd attacked the job with precision, determination, and complete success.

Yes, he was going to be an extremely thorough governor.

The End

* * * *

Also from 1001 Dark Nights and Jennifer Probst, discover *The Marriage Arrangement, Somehow, Some Way* and *Searching for Mine.*

* * * *

Curious about Chloe and Owen's story? Stay tuned for the next installment in the STAY series! Here's a peek:

Begin Again
A Stay Novella
By Jennifer Probst
Coming July 28, 2020

Chloe Lake is finally living her dream. As the daughter of the Governor, she's consistently in the spotlight, and after being dubbed the Most Eligible Bachelorette of NYC, both her career and personal life has exploded. Fortunately, her work as an advocate for animal welfare requires constant publicity and funding, so she embraces her role and plays for the camera—anything for the sake of her beloved rescues.

But when a big case is on the line, she's faced with the one obstacle she never counted on: the boy who broke her heart is back, and in order to gain justice, they need to work together.

Chloe swears she can handle it until old feelings resurface, and she's faced with a heartbreaking choice.

Will this time end differently—or are they destined to be only each other's first love—instead of forever?

Owen Salt fell hard for Chloe when he was a screwed-up kid in college, and spent the next years changing himself into the man his grandfather believed he was capable of. But when his career led him across the country, he knew he needed to leave the woman he loved behind. He's never forgotten her, but as the new darling of the press, now, she's way out of his league. When work brings him back to fight for justice by her side, he swears he can handle it.

But he's never really gotten over his first love—and he wants one more opportunity to prove he's a man who's worthy.

Can Owen convince the woman who holds his heart to take a second chance on forever—or is it too late for them both?

Sign up for the 1001 Dark Nights Newsletter
and be entered to win a Tiffany Key necklace.

There's a contest every month!

Go to www.1001DarkNights.com to subscribe.

**As a bonus, all subscribers can download
FIVE FREE exclusive books!**

Discover 1001 Dark Nights Collection Six

DRAGON CLAIMED by Donna Grant
A Dark Kings Novella

ASHES TO INK by Carrie Ann Ryan
A Montgomery Ink: Colorado Springs Novella

ENSNARED by Elisabeth Naughton
An Eternal Guardians Novella

EVERMORE by Corinne Michaels
A Salvation Series Novella

VENGEANCE by Rebecca Zanetti
A Dark Protectors/Rebels Novella

ELI'S TRIUMPH by Joanna Wylde
A Reapers MC Novella

CIPHER by Larissa Ione
A Demonica Underworld Novella

RESCUING MACIE by Susan Stoker
A Delta Force Heroes Novella

ENCHANTED by Lexi Blake
A Masters and Mercenaries Novella

TAKE THE BRIDE by Carly Phillips
A Knight Brothers Novella

INDULGE ME by J. Kenner
A Stark Ever After Novella

THE KING by Jennifer L. Armentrout
A Wicked Novella

QUIET MAN by Kristen Ashley
A Dream Man Novella

ABANDON by Rachel Van Dyken
A Seaside Pictures Novella

THE OPEN DOOR by Laurelin Paige
A Found Duet Novella

CLOSER by Kylie Scott
A Stage Dive Novella

SOMETHING JUST LIKE THIS by Jennifer Probst
A Stay Novella

BLOOD NIGHT by Heather Graham
A Krewe of Hunters Novella

TWIST OF FATE by Jill Shalvis
A Heartbreaker Bay Novella

MORE THAN PLEASURE YOU by Shayla Black
A More Than Words Novella

WONDER WITH ME by Kristen Proby
A With Me In Seattle Novella

THE DARKEST ASSASSIN by Gena Showalter
A Lords of the Underworld Novella

Also from 1001 Dark Nights:
DAMIEN by J. Kenner

Discover More Jennifer Probst

The Marriage Arrangement
A Marriage to a Billionaire Novella

She had run from her demons...

Caterina Victoria Windsor fled her family winery after a humiliating broken engagement, and spent the past year in Italy rebuilding her world. But when Ripley Savage shows up with a plan to bring her back home, and an outrageous demand for her to marry him, she has no choice but to return to face her past. But when simple attraction begins to run deeper, Cat has to decide if she's strong enough to trust again...and strong enough to stay...

He vowed to bring her back home to be his wife...

Rip Savage saved Windsor Winery, but the only way to make it truly his is to marry into the family. He's not about to walk away from the only thing he's ever wanted, even if he has to tame the spoiled brat who left her legacy and her father behind without a care. When he convinces her to agree to a marriage arrangement and return home, he never counted on the fierce sexual attraction between them to grow into something more. But when deeper emotions emerge, Rip has to fight for something he wants even more than Winsor Winery: his future wife.

* * * *

Somehow, Some Way
A Billionaire Builders Novella

Bolivar Randy Heart (aka Brady) knows exactly what he wants next in life: the perfect wife. Raised in a strict traditional family household, he seeks a woman who is sweet, conservative, and eager to settle down. With his well-known protective and dominant streak, he needs a woman to offer him balance in a world where he relishes control.

Too bad the newly hired, gorgeous, rehab addict is blasting through all his preconceptions and wrecking his ideals...one nail at a time...

Charlotte Grayson knows who she is and refuses to apologize. Growing up poor made her appreciate the simple things in life, and her new job at Pierce Brothers Construction is perfect to help her carve out a career in renovating houses. When an opportunity to transform a dilapidated house in a dangerous neighborhood pops up, she goes in full throttle. Unfortunately, she's forced to work with the firm's sexy architect who's driving her crazy with his archaic views on women.

Too bad he's beginning to tempt her to take a chance on more than just work...one stroke at a time...

Somehow, some way, they need to work together to renovate a house without killing each other...or surrendering to the white-hot chemistry knocking at the front door.

* * * *

Searching for Mine
A Searching For Novella

The Ultimate Anti-Hero Meets His Match...

Connor Dunkle knows what he wants in a woman, and it's the three B's. Beauty. Body. Boobs. Other women need not apply. With his good looks and easygoing charm, he's used to getting what he wants—and who. Until he comes face to face with the one woman who's slowly making his life hell...and enjoying every moment...

Ella Blake is a single mom and a professor at the local Verily College who's climbed up the ranks the hard way. Her ten-year-old son is a constant challenge, and her students are driving her crazy—namely Connor Dunkle, who's failing her class and trying to charm his way into a better grade. Fuming at his chauvinistic tendencies, Ella teaches him the ultimate lesson by giving him a *special* project to help his grade. When sparks fly, neither of them are ready to face their true feelings, but will love teach them the ultimate lesson of all?

About Jennifer Probst

Jennifer Probst wrote her first book at twelve years old. She bound it in a folder, read it to her classmates, and hasn't stopped writing since. She holds a masters in English Literature and lives in the beautiful Hudson Valley in upstate New York. Her family keeps her active, stressed, joyous, and sad her house will never be truly clean. Her passions include horse racing, Scrabble, rescue dogs, Italian food, and wine—not necessarily in that order.

She is the New York Times, USA Today, and Wall Street Journal bestselling author of sexy and erotic contemporary romance. She was thrilled her book, The Marriage Bargain, spent 26 weeks on the New York Times. Her work has been translated in over a dozen countries, sold over a million copies, and was dubbed a "romance phenom" by Kirkus Reviews. She is also a proud three-time RITA finalist.

She loves hearing from readers. Visit her website for updates on new releases and her street team at www.jenniferprobst.com.

Discover 1001 Dark Nights

COLLECTION ONE
FOREVER WICKED by Shayla Black
CRIMSON TWILIGHT by Heather Graham
CAPTURED IN SURRENDER by Liliana Hart
SILENT BITE: A SCANGUARDS WEDDING by Tina Folsom
DUNGEON GAMES by Lexi Blake
AZAGOTH by Larissa Ione
NEED YOU NOW by Lisa Renee Jones
SHOW ME, BABY by Cherise Sinclair
ROPED IN by Lorelei James
TEMPTED BY MIDNIGHT by Lara Adrian
THE FLAME by Christopher Rice
CARESS OF DARKNESS by Julie Kenner

COLLECTION TWO
WICKED WOLF by Carrie Ann Ryan
WHEN IRISH EYES ARE HAUNTING by Heather Graham
EASY WITH YOU by Kristen Proby
MASTER OF FREEDOM by Cherise Sinclair
CARESS OF PLEASURE by Julie Kenner
ADORED by Lexi Blake
HADES by Larissa Ione
RAVAGED by Elisabeth Naughton
DREAM OF YOU by Jennifer L. Armentrout
STRIPPED DOWN by Lorelei James
RAGE/KILLIAN by Alexandra Ivy/Laura Wright
DRAGON KING by Donna Grant
PURE WICKED by Shayla Black
HARD AS STEEL by Laura Kaye
STROKE OF MIDNIGHT by Lara Adrian
ALL HALLOWS EVE by Heather Graham
KISS THE FLAME by Christopher Rice
DARING HER LOVE by Melissa Foster
TEASED by Rebecca Zanetti
THE PROMISE OF SURRENDER by Liliana Hart

COLLECTION THREE

HIDDEN INK by Carrie Ann Ryan
BLOOD ON THE BAYOU by Heather Graham
SEARCHING FOR MINE by Jennifer Probst
DANCE OF DESIRE by Christopher Rice
ROUGH RHYTHM by Tessa Bailey
DEVOTED by Lexi Blake
Z by Larissa Ione
FALLING UNDER YOU by Laurelin Paige
EASY FOR KEEPS by Kristen Proby
UNCHAINED by Elisabeth Naughton
HARD TO SERVE by Laura Kaye
DRAGON FEVER by Donna Grant
KAYDEN/SIMON by Alexandra Ivy/Laura Wright
STRUNG UP by Lorelei James
MIDNIGHT UNTAMED by Lara Adrian
TRICKED by Rebecca Zanetti
DIRTY WICKED by Shayla Black
THE ONLY ONE by Lauren Blakely
SWEET SURRENDER by Liliana Hart

COLLECTION FOUR
ROCK CHICK REAWAKENING by Kristen Ashley
ADORING INK by Carrie Ann Ryan
SWEET RIVALRY by K. Bromberg
SHADE'S LADY by Joanna Wylde
RAZR by Larissa Ione
ARRANGED by Lexi Blake
TANGLED by Rebecca Zanetti
HOLD ME by J. Kenner
SOMEHOW, SOME WAY by Jennifer Probst
TOO CLOSE TO CALL by Tessa Bailey
HUNTED by Elisabeth Naughton
EYES ON YOU by Laura Kaye
BLADE by Alexandra Ivy/Laura Wright
DRAGON BURN by Donna Grant
TRIPPED OUT by Lorelei James
STUD FINDER by Lauren Blakely
MIDNIGHT UNLEASHED by Lara Adrian
HALLOW BE THE HAUNT by Heather Graham

On Behalf of 1001 Dark Nights,

Liz Berry and M.J. Rose would like to thank ~

Steve Berry
Doug Scofield
Kim Guidroz
Jillian Stein
InkSlinger PR
Dan Slater
Asha Hossain
Chris Graham
Chelle Olson
Kasi Alexander
Jessica Johns
Dylan Stockton
Richard Blake
and Simon Lipskar

Made in the USA
Monee, IL
23 November 2019